The Long Winter

of 1880-81

What was it Really Like?

By Dan L. White

The Long Hard Winter of 1880-81

Published by Ashley Preston Publishing
Hartville, Mo. 65667

www.danlwhitebooks.com

Cover design by Carrie A. Gaffney.
Photograph by Elmer and Tenney, *Snow Blockade*, Southern Minnesota Division, Chicago, Milwaukee and St. Paul Railway.

Copyright ©2011 by Dan L. White.
All rights reserved. Printed in the United States of America. No part of this book may be reproduced in any form or by any means, electronic, mechanical, photocopying, scanning, or otherwise, without permission in writing from the publisher, except by a reviewer who may quote brief passages in a review.

Little House is a registered trademark of HarperCollins Publishers Inc.

ISBN 13: 978-1466477681
ISBN 10: 1466477687

Also available in digital format.

Table of Contents

1. The Black, Hard, Long, Snow Winter, 5

2. The Awful Autumn Blizzard, 13

3. The Big Blow, 29

4. Blizzard at School, 37

5. Train Trouble, 49

6. Spring?, 77

7. The Thaw, 91

8. The Long, Hard, Black, Snow, Flood, Whatever Winter, 105

Endnotes, 137

Other Books by Dan L. White, 145

Other books by Dan L. White
See page 145 for descriptions

Laura's Love Story
The lifetime love of Laura Ingalls and Almanzo Wilder

Laura Ingalls' Friends Remember Her

Devotionals with Laura

Laura Ingalls Wilder's Most inspiring Writings

Big Bible Lessons from Laura Ingalls' Little Books

The Real Laura Ingalls
Who was Real, What was Real on her Prairie TV Show

Reading along with Laura Ingalls in the Big Wisconsin Woods

Reading along with Laura Ingalls at her Kansas Prairie Home

The Jubilee Principle: *God's Plan for Economic Freedom*

Homeschool Happenings, Happenstance and Happiness
A Light Look at Homeschool Life

Tebows' Homeschooled! Should You?

School Baals
How an Old Idol with a New Name Sneaked into Your School

Life Lessons from Jane Austen's Pride and Prejudice
From her book, her characters and her Bible

Daring to Love like God: *Marriage as a Spiritual Union*

Wifely Wisdom for Sometimes Foolish Husbands
From Laura Ingalls to Almanzo and Abigail to Nabal

Chapter 1

The Black, Hard, Long, Snow Winter

When you wonder if the winter of 1880-81 was as bad as Laura Ingalls Wilder wrote in her book *The Long Winter*, remember this –

that was the year the word "blizzard" came into common use.

Laura Ingalls Wilder wrote nine Little House® books, from which the famous television program *Little House on the Prairie* was taken. The sixth book in that series was *The Long Winter*, a tale of nonstop blizzards on the prairies of Dakota Territory in the winter of 1880-81.

And during that winter, "blizzard" blew its way into the English language.

The *Online Etymology Dictionary* explains:

> "blizzard – 1859, origin obscure (perhaps somehow connected with blaze (1)); it came into general use in the U.S. in the hard winter 1880-81, though it was used with a sense of "violent blow" in Amer. Eng., 1829; and blizz "violent rainstorm" is attested from 1770."[1]

Houghton Mifflin Word Origins discusses the change in the meaning of blizzard from human violence to violent weather.

"In frontier territory, blizzard was "a knock-down blow," delivered at first by a fist or gun rather than by the weather. It must have been in use by the mid-1820s. We encounter it in an 1829 glossary in the Virginia Literary Museum: "Blizzard. 'A violent blow,' perhaps from [German] Blitz, lightning. Kentucky." Whatever its origin, the word was familiar to frontiersman Davy Crockett, who wrote in his 1835 Tour Down East that at dinner, asked by a parson for a toast, "Not knowing whether he intended to have some fun at my expense, I concluded to go ahead and give him and his likes a blizzard." In this case it was a blizzard of words.

Blizzard went to college too. A writer in 1881 recalled, "In 1836 I first heard the word 'blizzard' among the young men at Illinois College, Jacksonville. If one struck a ball a severe blow in playing town-ball it would be said 'That's a blizzard.'"

Meanwhile, back on the frontier, blizzard began to be the term for the severe blow struck by a snowstorm. An 1862 book called Forty Years on the Frontier recorded this entry: "Snowed in the forenoon. Very cold in afternoon. Raw east wind. Everybody went to grand ball given by John Grant at Grantsville and a severe blizzard blew up and raged all night. We danced all night; no outside storm could dampen the festivities."

During the particularly severe winter of 1880-81, this kind of blizzard struck the whole country, as a writer in the Nation of New York City commented in 1881: "The hard weather has called into use a word which promises to become a national Americanism, namely 'blizzard.' It designates a storm (of snow and wind) which men cannot resist away from shelter."

In general usage ever since, the blizzard of snow has knocked out the former meaning of mere human violence."[2]

Why did the word blizzard blow itself into the English language that year? Because more than any year in recent history, the winter of 1880-81 was the year of blizzards.

That winter had several names.

In Nebraska, it was called the Black Winter, as in a 1919 article from *The History of Custer County Nebraska* titled "The Black Winter of 1880-81:"

> "The winter of 1880-81 will never be forgotten by those engaged in the cattle business in Custer county. Men who in the beginning of that winter were wealthy, found themselves bankrupt in the spring.
>
> ...The following spring many who had engaged in the business in Custer county, and who until this winter had believed there was no grazing country equal to it, quit the business in disgust and left the county. Nothing like this winter had preceded it in the history of the country, and nothing like it has been experienced since."[3]

For many others, that winter was known as the Snow Winter.

> "Out on the prairie during the pioneer period, settlers named only the really bad winters. The worst of all was just called the "Snow Winter." "Today children read Laura Ingalls Wilder's classic novel "The Long Winter" as a thrilling story of the old days -- but in fact every detail in the book matches up with pioneer memories of the Snow Winter. There have been colder winters on the prairie and deadlier blizzards, but for sheer

volume and duration of snow, that Snow Winter has never been rivaled."[4]

Edward Jensen, the first Norwegian settler in Grant County, South Dakota also wrote about the Snow Winter.

"Then there was the snow winter of 1880-1. The snow came on the 15th of October and did not leave until the middle of April. The winter came before we were ready for it. We had not ground our grain nor had we made our purchases. As well, we had no closer town than Canby, Minn. and to the nearest mill it was 50-60 miles."[5]

Over on the eastern edge of Wisconsin, the *Milwaukee Journal* ran an article on October 15, 1922 that was headlined, "Fall Blizzard 42 Years Ago Began 'Winter of the Big Snow.'" The story explained:

"The storm was the forerunner of the most severe winter in the memory of living generations – the winter of the big snow. All through Wisconsin and northern Michigan, when tales of storms are going the rounds, the story of the big snow is sure to be told. Such an impression did it leave on the minds of people at that time, for many years after events were dated from "the year of the big snow.""[6]

Laura's book *The Long Winter* was set in southern Dakota Territory, or what in 1889 became the state of South Dakota. That winter was known in the area as the Hard Winter. The *Weekly South Dakotan* said about that period:

"Snow was something Dakotans soon knew a lot about. The Hard Winter of 1880-1881 took many by surprise. Temperatures hovered below zero for weeks."[7]

Laura herself said that the locals in South Dakota called it, not the long winter, but the Hard Winter.

> *"In a late issue of a St. Louis paper, I find the following,"* she wrote in 1917. *"Experts in the office of home economics of the United States Department of Agriculture have found it is possible to grind whole wheat in an ordinary coffee mill fine enough for use as a breakfast cereal and even fine enough for use in bread making.*
>
> *If the experts of the Department of Agriculture had asked any one of the 200 people who spent the winter of 1880-81 in De Smet, S. Dak., they might have saved themselves the trouble of experimenting. I think, myself, that it is rather a joke on our experts at Washington to be 36 years behind the times.*
>
> *That winter, known still among the old residents as "the hard winter," we demonstrated that wheat could be ground in an ordinary coffee mill and used for bread making. Prepared in that way it was the staff of life for the whole community. The grinding at home was not done to reduce the cost of living, but simply to make living possible."*[8]

In fact, Laura originally titled her book *The Hard Winter*. Her publisher changed the name to *The Long Winter*. The book was for children, and *The Long Winter* doesn't sound as glum as *The Hard Winter*.

Either way, hard winter or long winter –

It was a long, hard winter.

Was that winter as hard as Laura pictured in her book?

Perhaps not.

Laura first recorded the story of her life as a girl on the prairie in a manuscript titled *Pioneer Girl*. Her daughter Rose was a nationally famous writer and Rose tried to place Laura's story with magazine and book publishers. They refused the manuscript.

That's hard for us to believe today. Laura Ingalls Wilder couldn't get her book published?

Laura's life was a great story, but *Pioneer Girl* didn't show it. The manuscript was written more in a straightforward fashion than as a novel, as if Laura was just sitting across the table casually chatting about old times. *Pioneer Girl* told the story but it did not show the story.

To be successful, the book had to have not just facts but drama. If the story wasn't compelling, the book would never get published, particularly during the Great Depression of the thirties, when publishers had trouble selling their products. Therefore, Laura adjusted some of the facts of her life to better shape her stories.

Such as –

Laura lived in the big woods of Wisconsin both before and after she lived in the little house on the prairie in Kansas. The books only show her living in Wisconsin before Kansas.

The books completely left out the years that the Ingalls lived in Burr Oak, Iowa, where the only Ingalls son died.

The books shorten the age difference between Laura and her beau and eventual husband Almanzo from ten years to six.

Okay, so Laura changed a few things. Her prime purpose was to write a good story, based on the real facts of her life, but embellished and shaped to make it compelling. Naturally she had no idea that her writing would be so widely read and every detail pored over by thousands and thousands of people. She even said that when she was writing her books, she had no idea she was writing history![9] She thought she was just writing children's stories!

When she wrote *The Long Winter*, Laura based it on her real experience, but she was not a historian and did not match every last detail with actual history. That would have been very difficult, anyway, because records on the frontier from that time were scant, and she was remembering events that had occurred more than half a century before she wrote them down.

Laura's friend Neta Seal spoke of how Laura remembered remembering.

> *"She said a lot of nights when she'd go to bed, she'd wake up and some of the things would be coming to her and she'd get up and start writing. Sometimes maybe she'd write as it kept coming, unfolding as she wrote. She would write maybe till the wee hours of the morning. When she got tired, she'd go over there and lay down on that couch. You know, that old fashioned settee that's in the room.*
>
> *Almanzo would get up and she was sleeping, and he'd never wake her up. He'd go on about the chores."*[10]

Laura had to slowly dredge up her memories from long ago. As with any of us, they would not be perfectly accurate. Someone has dubiously calculated that she mentions thirty-five different blizzards during the long winter.[11] If there were thirty-five blizzards in seven months, or about 210 days, that is a blizzard every six days, more than a blizzard a week for thirty weeks. In reality, it would have been impossible for Laura even to remember thirty-five different blizzards sixty years later. Ask your grandma what she remembers from sixty years ago and you will get a pregnant pause, even though she is a grandma.

Therefore we will accept that not every historical meteorological detail, day by day and degree by degree and blizzard by blizzard, has to match Laura's book. She was primarily telling a children's story, not compiling history.

However, the story that she told actually was based on the reality of her life, as she remembered it. Laura Ingalls Wilder told a shockingly incredible story about the winter of 1880-81, the year she turned fourteen years old, the year the little town on the prairie nearly starved and the year her future husband Almanzo risked his life to find wheat for the townspeople, including cute little Laura Ingalls.

Was that winter really that different? Or was it just an ordinary winter for back then, when the snows came often and heavy, and people ice-skated every year on frozen rivers and ponds, because winters were simply colder at that time?

What was the long winter really like?

~~~~~

Chapter 2

The Awful Autumn Blizzard

The Long Winter, the novel, begins with Laura helping Pa Ingalls put up hay. Ma Ingalls did not think young ladies should work outside in the fields. She and Pa had no living sons, though, to help with the hard outside work. Once they did have a son, Charles Frederick Ingalls, born on November 1, 1875, almost nine years younger than Laura. But he died on August 27 of the next year, only about ten months old.

Mary was the oldest girl, and she might have been the one helping in the hay, except she had been stricken blind from an illness in 1879 when she was fourteen. Mary did help with the inside work, by remembering where everything was in the little house, but she was not able to help outside, on the endless prairie. Anyway, Mary always preferred working indoors.

On the other hand, Laura loved being outdoors. So Laura, who was thirteen years old but still small, helped Pa with the hay. He threw the hay up on the wagon and she tromped it down with her feet. Then they carried the hay to where they stacked it and Laura spread the hay out in the bottom of the stack.

After her first day of haying, Laura hurt so badly that she cried, but only to herself. She did not want to complain.

Homesteading on the frontier was very tough. Beatrice Wade Sipher's family homesteaded several miles east of Bancroft, South Dakota, only about ten miles from the Ingalls homestead. They arrived in 1883, two years after the long winter, and Beatrice kept a journal of her experiences.

"Father, Mother, my brother Marvilla, and I came by train to the frontier settlement of DeSmet, in May of 1883. We put up at a hotel and Father hired a man and team to show him the vacant land. Father filed on 160 acres of land and we came to live on it seven years. He later proved his land and got the title. Father built a small frame house and covered it with tar paper. Next, he built a sod barn, and chicken house.

The prairie grass was very luxuriant and all over the prairie it was up to my knees. Lots of prairie chickens and ducks lived near the sloughs. The first eggs we had to eat were some Marvilla found in a duck's nest. She was not setting yet so the temptation was great. There were nests all around the sloughs. There was not much variety in food, with the country being new.

Father bought a cow "Polly" and calf by her side and one hen from James Clewett. I called the hen Pinky, and we kept her for many years. He managed to buy five hens from five different places, as nobody wanted to sell any. Father was traveling around on foot trying to find what he wanted. From Mr. Boast, he got a cow we called Dinah. We had two cows, two oxen, five chickens, and one heifer calf that first year.

My older brother, Bartholomew came out to Dakota Territory in the fall and filed on 80 acres that joined Father's, but didn't like it. The prairie was too lonesome for him. He stayed only one winter. He used to pace the floor and played his concertina for hours. He could see nothing but snow and a few shanties, some with smoke coming out of the chimneys. We could see for miles, and could count the cars when the trains went between DeSmet and Manchester. The track was seven miles south and sometimes the mirage would show several little villages. Bartholomew went back east to New York state the next spring."[12]

Beatrice's brother left South Dakota because in the winter he could see nothing but snow and a few claim shanties. That was not during the long, hard winter, but just a normal winter. Homesteading on the prairie frontier was tough, and when Laura cried because she hurt from haying, that was part of the frontier life.

But that hay was worth more than they knew. Laura and Pa made haystack after haystack. Only with Laura's help was Pa able to put up so much hay.

Why did Laura start the story of *The Long Winter* with putting up hay?

Because the hay that half-pint Laura helped put up saved their lives that winter.

The first chapter of *The Long Winter* also mentions Pa peering at a muskrat house that was far thicker than usual. In 1950, U. S. Senator Robert Kerr of Oklahoma wrote to Indian leaders in different states asking how they interpreted signs about the coming winter. Answers to his letter included this.

"The other response, from the Crow Agency in Montana, was informed by 70 year-old Sidney Blackhair. He had learned to forecast from his father, a famed Crow chieftain. He predicted a

mild winter for southeastern Montana and northern Wyoming, based on factors such as (1) the occurrence of a mid-September snowfall; (2) frequent rains; (3) ants not having gone into the ground yet; (4) snakes still being out; and (5) an absence of frogs. The letter writer, Joe Medicine Crow, said these signs had been observed "by the Indians of this region from time immemorial and are well founded and could be relied upon." He also said means of forecasting had been developed by Indians in other regions "for their particular locality."

It is not known how many letters Kerr sent in October 1951, but seven interesting responses were received, all from outside of Oklahoma. The Chippewa Tribe in Cass Lake, Minnesota, indicated that it would be a long and hard winter; signs included that "if the muskrat or beaver build an unusually high and large house, the winter will be severe." Others Chippewa signs included the heaviness of wild animal fur, the thickness of tree bark, and whether "squaw-corn" is heavily covered with shell."[13]

Big muskrat houses meant big winters. The thick muskrat house that Pa examined was a sign of the winter that was to come.

Not everybody who homesteaded in Dakota Territory decided to winter there. Some worked the land during the summer, then skedaddled back to settled country for the winter.

"In 1878 two young men, about twenty years of age came from Watertown, Wisconsin to Watertown, Dakota Territory. They walked over one hundred miles to the southeast part of Putney Township where they staked their claim, deciding that it was the best tillable land within the distance. They checked the

depth of the black loam as they traveled northwest of Watertown, Dakota Territory. Each winter was spent in Wisconsin and not until 1882 did they bring their wives with them. They were Joe S. Schornack and Gustav Lietz."[14]

By deciding to winter back in Wisconsin, those young men did not totally miss the hard winter of 1880-81, but at least they were back where they had food and fuel so they could eat and stay warm.

The previous winter, 1879-80, the Ingalls had stayed in a surveyors' house owned by the railroad. It was small but snug and well supplied and they were comfortable there, as told in *By the Shores of Silver Lake*. After that pleasant winter, in the autumn of 1880 Pa Ingalls and his family prepared to face again the winter in Dakota Territory.

It wasn't long in coming.

Laura recalled a hard freeze on the first of October. With that freeze, the haying was over and they gathered the garden produce. The Ingalls picked beans and tomatoes, and turnips and potatoes. Their harvest was small, because that was their first garden on the new homestead. Potatoes were their most abundant crop; they had five bushels to last through the next summer. Of course, they expected that they could buy more food throughout the winter and not have to survive only on those potatoes. That fall, though, Pa could not shoot geese for their meat because the birds skipped stopping on the Big Slough and hurried on south, ahead of the coming winter, as if they knew something.

Only about two weeks after the first freeze, as Laura went to sleep she heard rain pattering on the roof of the claim shanty. Then the next morning, Laura awoke with a cold nose, Pa was slapping his hands together to get them warm, and the wind was howling all around the very little house. It was an autumn blizzard.

The account of Laura's life in *Pioneer Girl* is not dramatized as it is in the subsequent books, and is a matter-of-fact record of Laura's memories. Here is how she described that blizzard in that manuscript.

> "When next I waked, Pa was building a fire and singing, "Oh I am as happy as a big sunflower that nods and bends in the breezes. And my heart is as light as the wind that blows and comes and goes as it pleases." I glanced at the window but it seemed to be covered with a whiteness I could not see through. When the fire was going good Ma got up, but when I started she told me to lie still. We were all to lie still under the covers for there was no use of our all being cold and there was an awful blizzard outside."

Laura recalled that the blizzard lasted all day and all night, then the next day and next night, and then on the next morning the shrieking wind let up a bit and the Ingalls could see a few feet outside their tarpaper shanty.

That early October blizzard that Laura recalled in *The Long Winter* was in fact one of the most noted blizzards in recent history, simply because it was so early.

Newspapers throughout the area reported that the October blizzard took everyone by surprise. In one example, three men were building a sod house near De Smet. They hauled in lumber for the roof and began to cut sod and stack the walls. When the walls were about half height rain began falling, so they quickly placed a temporary roof over the short walls and climbed in. They went to sleep that night in their half size house, expecting to finish the walls the next day. Overnight the rain turned to ice and the ice turned to snow, and by the next morning they were in the middle of a full fledged blizzard in a half fledged house. They rode out the long storm in their short house, snug in their squat little soddy.[15]

Such an early storm even made the history books. *The History of Dakota Territory* by George Kingsbury left this description for posterity.

> *"The winter of 1880-81 opened October 15th, 1880, with an unprecedented storm of snow, which assumed the magnitude and fierceness of a blizzard. It lasted about twenty-four hours, its only redeeming feature being that the temperature was not dangerously cold, though the Big Sioux, Vermillion and James rivers were frozen over. Railroad traffic was tied up by the heavy snow, which had drifted into and filled many of the cuts, and the telegraph lines were badly injured, caused by the weight of the damp snow, which clung to the wires in heavy masses and bore them to the ground. Live stock suffered severely, thousands of head being out on the prairies at the time, and the work of threshing was then under way all through the territory. A foot, and in some places more, of heavy snow fell....There were intelligent Indians then living at the Yankton Agency who had been born in this Upper Missouri Valley seventy-five and eighty years prior to this event who could recall no occurrence of such a wintry visitation during October. Heavy storms and destructive blizzards had been*

known late in the spring, but the rule for October, and even November, had been pleasant and autumn weather. It was a widespread and an unusually heavy storm even for midwinter, and the snowdrifts in the towns were of such prodigious size and extent as to blockade the streets and walks, and wagons and carts were employed to remove the immense accumulations before team traffic could be resumed and the thoroughfares made passable for pedestrians. Railway trains and telegraph lines were a week or ten days repairing and resuming business in an orderly manner..."[16]

John Stanley was a homesteader and newspaper editor in Gary, South Dakota, less than a hundred miles northeast of De Smet. In his autobiography, he also recalled this unseasonal blizzard.

"It was a glorious autumn season and we had the farm work well advanced, when on October 15th (1880), another date that is unforgettable, a drizzling rain was most acceptable to everybody. That evening, just as darkness was settling over the scene, our elder sister, Angela, and her husband, (she having been married in June of that year to William H. Donaldson, a land locator and real estate salesman), arrived to spend the night. There was no place to shelter their buggy and it was left outside. A new, long whip was left in its place in the buggy, its tip reaching several feet above the ground. It was a pleasant evening within that farm home, with the children all-present again and with the welcome rain pattering on the roof and against the windows.

Next morning a different scene covered the landscape, the rain having changed to wet snow, and the wind blowing terrifically-we were experiencing our first blizzard. So fierce was the storm of wind and snow that not a thing was visible outside.

The chores were not done as usual before breakfast. Fortunately our new brother-in-law was a native of the prairies of Minnesota, and was familiar with blizzards. When I was preparing to make an attempt to go to the stable to look after the stock he warned me against going out without tying a rope (clothesline) about my waist, with someone in the house to look after the other end of the line, so that in the event I failed to land at the stable I might be directed by the line back to the house.

I had the confidence of youth and really thought it was ridiculous to intimate that I couldn't run to the stable in a direct line, not over 100 feet eastward. However, following his advice, I permitted him to rope me and I made the run, but instead of reaching the stable I bumped against the familiar hitching post that was directly south of the house about 75 feet. I had not fully straightened out the clothesline, but realized I had gone wrong. I then made my way directly to the house without trouble.

Undaunted, I made another effort and suddenly dropped several feet, finding myself (feeling rather than seeing) between a snow bank and the stable - the wind having created an eddy that kept the snow from banking solidly against the stable. Fortunately the stable door was close by and I was able to enter.

The season's hay had been stacked outside only a few feet from the door, but the drifted snow had entirely covered it. Consequently the stock had to subsist on the straw (there being more than enough for all winter) with which the pole shed had been covered and surrounded. The shed was attached to the board stable and provided a good, large run-way for all the stock, they being loose therein, but had temporarily to do without water, the blizzard continuing all day and far into the night with no letup in its fury. Finding the stock all getting along nicely I returned to the house without difficulty.

Next morning dawned bright, clear and still. It was a strange, beautiful sight-far as the eye could reach the whole landscape seemed a level blanket of snow, every depression and ravine being filled-a strange new world, sparkling in the sunlight. The tip of that long buggy whip was the only evidence as to where the buggy stood - the snow having drifted around and entirely over the buggy. Those were the conditions under which the inhabitants of Dakota and the people west of the Mississippi and north of Southern Iowa were introduced to the winter season of 1880-81, and from that time forward for nearly six months winter reigned, not mildly but boisterously. The snow that fell in October remained to the end of the winter season."[17]

That Indian summer blizzard tore all across the upper Midwest. The *Milwaukee Journal*, in its October 15, 1922 article recalled the ferocity of that storm.

"Old Wisconsin residents will recall this week that 42 years ago – Oct. 16, 1880, to be exact – there swept down on the state from the North Platte valley in Nebraska a terrific storm of snow and sleet, borne of the wings of a 125-mile-an-hour gale. The unprecedented mid-fall blizzard covered an area 500 miles square in the north mid-west, covered parts of Nebraska, the Dakotas, Minnesota, Iowa, Wisconsin and northern

Michigan with several inches of snow, stalled hundreds of trains, caused untold suffering with its zero weather and unexpectedness, and churned Lake Michigan into a raging demon which wrecked or disabled practically every ship on its surface.

...On the morning of Oct. 16, 1880, the temperature dropped suddenly to 40 degrees above zero and later plunged to 27 above. Then a raw wind began to blow, bringing sleet and snow and increasing in force until it reached terrific speed. Near the source of the storm the wind blew as high as 125 miles an hour. In Milwaukee it reached a speed of 70 miles an hour.

...The snow fell to a depth of only several inches, but the wind drove it into high drifts and packed it into the railway cuts so hard that railway traffic was brought to a standstill all over the state. Rescue parties went out in sleighs carrying food to the stalled passenger trains. Windows in hundreds of homes in many cities and towns in the storm area were broken, adding to the discomfort."[18]

The Vermillion, South Dakota newspaper *Plain Talk* recalled this freak storm and severe winter many years later in 2009 in its "Sesquicentennial Highlights" of the town's history. After 129 years, that blizzard was still making headlines.

"The winter of 1880-81 was not only very severe but very long. It started in the middle of October and was going strong on the first of April, with very few mild days in between those dates. On Oct. 15 there were 12 to 15 inches of wet snow. Telegraph wires went down and there were no trains for three days. Thousands of head of livestock were reported lost."[19]

Yankton, South Dakota is south of De Smet, on the Nebraska border, and with seventy mile an hour winds from that storm, they might have thought they were going to blow into Nebraska.

> *"It was on this date, October 15 in 1880 that a violent early season blizzard raked Minnesota and the Dakotas. Winds gusted to 70 mph at Yankton SD, and snow drifts 10 to 15 feet high were reported in northwest Iowa and southeast South Dakota. Saint Paul MN reported a barometric pressure of 28.65 inches on the 16th. Railroads were blocked by drifts of snow which remained throughout the severe winter to follow."*[20]

In Minnesota, the October 16, 1880 storm is still listed as the earliest blizzard ever to hit that state. The winds drove the snow into drifts as high as twenty feet, as tall as a two-story building, and the snow stayed until the next spring.

Almanzo Wilder, Laura's husband, had a sister, Eliza Jane Wilder, who also had a homestead near De Smet. She was the teacher that Laura wrote her lazy, lousy Liza Jane poem about in *Little Town on the Prairie*. Eliza Jane wrote a letter to the land commissioner about the October blizzard.

> *"In Oct. a blizzard came and for three days we could not see an object ten ft from us. The R.R. were blocked for ten days. Snow in the cuts being packed like ice. After the storm ceased I went to town for flour and coal.*
>
> *Our merchants had none. A carload of flour would have been there in a few hours when blockaded.*

> *My mother took me home with her for the winter. But I left everything except my wardrobe in Dakota not expecting to be gone more than two or three months. But storm followed storm. After the middle of December I think no trains reached De Smet until May.*
>
> *Many families were reported frozen to death and others lived wholly on turnips, some on wheat ground in a coffee mill."*[21]

Eliza Jane was fortunate to have spent the winter with her parents in Minnesota. They still got the blizzards there, but they were not on the western frontier and therefore were not cut off from food and fuel.

Around the time of Groundhog Day in 2011, a blizzard covered about a third of the United States. This particular storm affected about a hundred million people, many major cities were completely shut down, and several states declared states of emergency – yet that blizzard, as it moved across the nation, only lasted one day in any given area. The October blizzard of 1880 lasted three days, with the wind ceaselessly blowing the snow that was falling and had fallen.

After the storm, Laura wrote of seeing cattle that seemed frozen in their spots, unable to move.

> *"They did not seem like real cattle. They stood so terribly still. In the whole herd there was not the least movement. Only their breathing sucked their hairy sides in between the rib bones and pushed them out again. Their hip bones and their shoulder bones stood up sharply. Their legs were braced out, stiff and still. And where their heads should be, swollen white lumps seemed fast to the ground under the blowing snow."*[22]

Those cattle looked as if they were frozen to the ground, held fast by the ice and snow that had imprisoned them in place as they stood with their backs to the storm.

In *Pioneer Girl*, Laura said that *"their breath and the snow, blown into their eyelashes and the hair around their eyes, had formed ice over their eyes until they could not see at all."*

The Lincoln, Nebraska article about *The Black Winter* mentioned in Chapter 1 talked about the rain turning into inverted icicles.

"Early in the winter a rain began falling. The grass became thoroughly saturated; then it suddenly turned cold, and every stalk, spear and blade of grass at once became an icicle — all matted together in one sheet of solid ice. Immediately following this came a heavy snow, from ten to twelve inches deep, which was again followed by another rain, and this in turn by another sudden cold wave, the result of which was to cover the surface of the snow with a thick, strong crust. The country was covered with ice and snow until spring. The winter was very severe, the temperature ranging for days and weeks at from ten to twenty below zero.

The conditions were such that it was almost impossible for the cattle to get to the grass. The winds, which ordinarily blew the snow off the hills and left the grass thereon free to the cattle, could not affect this solid body of ice and snow. The legs of the cattle, traveling about in a famished condition seeking food, soon became bruised and bleeding from contact with the sharp crust on the snow. There was plenty of feed on the ground, but the cattle could not get at it. They died by the hundreds and thousands. It was estimated that from seventy-five to ninety per cent of the cows and calves on the range perished that winter and sixty per cent of the steers also perished. They lay in piles behind the hills where they had sought shelter."

Even the cattle were to be pitied during that winter. Pa broke the ice off the animals whose eyes were iced over, one by one for twenty-five head. They bellowed and moved only a few steps. They were too tired to leave. By the next day they had trudged on, but then probably died that winter. The October blizzard was only the beginning of their troubles, because the October blizzard was only the beginning of the hard winter.

~~~~~

Chapter 3

The Big Blow

The October blizzard, once it moved over the Great Lakes, was not called The Big Snow, but was known as The Big Blow. Sailors also called it The Alpena Storm.

> *"The Alpena is undoubtedly one of the most famous shipwrecks on the east shore of Lake Michigan. She disappeared in October 1880 during a storm known as "The Big Blow" due to the devastation it caused throughout the Great Lakes."*[23]

In the late summer of 1880, the steamship Alpena was dry docked in Milwaukee for repairs to her rudder chain. Out of the water, she looked even bigger than when she rode the waves, as she stretched for two-thirds of a football field. Two big, powerful paddle wheels graced her sides like earrings.

> *"The Goodrich side wheel steamer Alpena was built by Thomas Arnold of Gallagher & Company at Marine City, Michigan in 1866. She was 197 feet in length, with a 26.66 foot beam, a depth of 12 feet and was rated at 654 tons. The wood-hulled steamer was powered by a single cylinder, vertical beam engine which drove a pair of 24' radius side wheels."*[24]

She was a beautiful ship, one of the best on Lake Michigan, and was described as a "white swan on the water."[25] Her regular run was between Chicago, Illinois and Muskegon, Michigan, with stops in Milwaukee, Wisconsin and other ports.

After being put back in the water, the ship sailed east from Chicago to Michigan, completing her run without incident. Then, on October 15, 1880, she began the return trip.

The Gooderich Line owned and operated the ship. The only list of passengers who were on board was kept onboard, so the number of passengers and crew was never exactly determined.

> *"The crew was 30 strong. It was stated, when the vessel left Muskegon that she had 70 passengers and took five at Grand Haven, mostly women. Gooderich thinks, however, that the passengers did not exceed 25 or perhaps 20."*[26]

The night that the Alpena began her journey into history was just a pleasant autumn evening.

> *"The Alpena left Grand Haven, Michigan bound for Chicago on Friday evening, October 15, 1880 at 9:30 PM. The weather was beautiful -- Indian Summer like. But the barometer was indicating a storm was coming and storm signals were out. She was met on her southwest journey by the steamer Muskegon at about 1:00 AM and everything seemed normal."*[27]

As the Alpena churned the dark waters of Lake Michigan heading west, the October blizzard headed east.

> *"The next day, October 16, 1880, the wind from Nebraska appeared around the Alpena as an early morning squall. By that afternoon the squall had turned into a hurricane and when darkness came, the storm rose to a shrieking fury. The temperature dropped suddenly to 27 degrees below zero and*

sleet and snow lashed the Alpena. Captain Napier stayed at the rudder of his sturdy ship, guiding her through the storm. He was concerned, but he was also confident that he could steer her through to Milwaukee."[28]

The storm that Captain Napier thought he could steer through was called the worst storm ever recorded on Lake Michigan. Some figured the winds of the storm at over a hundred miles an hour.

"At about 3:00 AM Saturday, October 16, 1880 the "worst gale in Lake Michigan recorded history" swept across the lake. The Alpena was seen at 6:00 AM, 7:00 AM and at 8:00 AM by the schooner Irish and by Captain George Boomsluiter of the barge City of Grand Haven about 35 miles off Kenosha, Wisconsin, laboring heavily in the high seas."[29]

The book *Great Lakes Shipwrecks & Survivals* gives more details about that voyage.

"The date was October 15, 1880, the weather pleasant, the sun shining, the thermometer ranging between sixty and seventy degrees. Light southerly winds prevailed over Lake Michigan. The Alpena coasts along the east shore paying a call at Muskegon and then putting in at Grand Haven a little further down the Lake, where she took on two carloads of apples and more passengers.

Counting new ticket holders, the steamer may have carried a total of 101 persons when she cleared Grand Haven early in the evening and cut across the Lake for Chicago, 108 miles away. Captain Nelson Napier, a veteran sailing master, noted a shift in wind and a fast tumble in barometric pressure, sure indications of an oncoming storm, but he took his chances on being off the Lake before the worst of it hit.

The Alpena was sighted by other vessels several times before midnight, proceeding on course and with no trouble, although the seas had begun to kick up. At midnight a violent southwesterly gale struck Lake Michigan with savage bursts of cyclonic fury. Temperatures dropped below freezing. Snow squalls rattled Chicago windows. Sometime between midnight and dawn the Alpena must have broken up and gone to the bottom in a storm that wrecked or badly damaged ninety other vessels."[30]

The captain of another ship saw the Alpena lose her battle with the blizzard.

"The ship Hattie Wells, captained by John Dearkoff, tossed and turned near the Alpena as the storm grew worse, and Captain Dearkoff decided to run for the harbor at Milwaukee. Later, he said he thought that was what the Alpena would do, but apparently Captain Napier had something different in mind. By now, the wind had formed a giant sledgehammer battering the Alpena and Captain Napier decided that he could not make Milwaukee, even though he was about halfway through his regular run.

"I don't know why he didn't head for Milwaukee like I headed for Milwaukee," Captain Dearkoff of the Hattie Wells said in his eyewitness account of the incident. "Me and my crew stood on deck and watched him try to turn his ship around in that storm. She was halfway around and that wind just took right hold of her and turned her over. She was swamped and she sank and we couldn't do a thing about it. We watched her disappear under the waves."[31]

When she did not show up on time, people waiting on shore feared the worst. Soon those fears were confirmed.

> "The storm had torn the Alpena apart so badly that bodies and wreckage were scattered along the beach for seventy miles – fire buckets with the name of the steamboat stenciled on them, a piano with the lid torn off, a fragment of stairway, cabin doors, life preservers, and apples bobbing in the surf and rolling up on the sand."[32]

Hundreds of people walked the shore searching for items from the ship that had washed up, including bodies.

On Oct. 19, the *Daily News' Grand Haven* reported,

> "A large quantity of freight from the Alpena has come ashore six miles south of here. Hundreds of citizens are now on the beach hunting for pieces of the wreck or possibly bodies. Several chests known to belong to the Alpena have been found north of Holland. It is thought that no one survived the wreck."[33]

A page from a diary was found, whose ending entry was written just before the end of the ship.

> "Holland, Mich., Oct. 21. -- Prof. Scott of Hope Collage, has a leaf from a diary found attached to a moulding of the cabin of the steamer ALPENA by a small nail. It is badly chafed and water-soaked, but by the aid of a glass it can be read as follows: "Oh, this is terrible! The steamer is breaking up fast. I am aboard from Grand Haven to Chicago. Geo, Connor." The last two letters of the name are very faint and may be Connell."[34]

Finally the Alpena's hull washed up. And her piano.

"The wreck is complete. She is broken into small fragments. The stern part of her hull lies near the harbor. The whole coast for 20 miles is strewn with the debris, freight, etc." The largest piece to land near Holland was the piano, "it being barely able to float, our sailors concluded that she did not come very far. And the arrival of other heavy pieces of the wreck would seem to corroborate this."

The Saugatuck Commercial Record newspaper reported shingles, lath, lumber and other pieces of the ill-fated Alpena were scattered thickly on the shore there. It was also reported that thousands of apples were found bobbing in the surf at Saugatuck.

No exact count of the victims is available, though the Holland City News stated 80 souls were lost."[35]

So the October blizzard became the Alpena Storm, but that ship was not at all the only one that went down.

"The Alpena Storm, as it came to be known, was the worst Lake Michigan storm on record up to 1880. Ninety boats wrecked during this two-day period. The lighthouse keeper on Pilot Island near the Door Peninsula, Emanuel Davidson, reported that the water around the island was white for a week after the storm. It was his belief that the severity of the storm had stirred the limestone of the lake bottom to such a degree that it mixed with the lake water.

Lake Michigan bore the brunt of the storm, although Lake Huron took a beating, too. While storms of greater intensity have occasionally swept across the entire Great Lakes basin, few have struck Lake Michigan with the fury of the Alpena Storm of 1880."[36]

The October Blizzard and the Alpena storm – that one storm alone was enough to make a memorable winter. But there were more memories to come from that winter.

~~~~~

Chapter 4

Blizzard at School

The October Blizzard was so-called simply because blizzards were not supposed to come in October. That was <u>the</u> October Blizzard.

A claim shanty like Pa's was built as hurriedly and cheaply as possible so that the homesteader had a home on his claim as the government required. Such a house could be built quickly for about a hundred dollars.

> *"A claim shanty usually consisted of one or two rooms with an attic where the children slept. The bed had a sack of straw or corn husks for a mattress. If the settlers came from the "old country," they usually had a feather bed or two; one to put over them and one under them to keep them warm during the cold winter nights. The rooms were very crowded and children often had to sleep on the floor. Sometimes there were five children in one bed. Many pioneers put a sack of straw under the bed and pulled it out at night. The table was usually homemade and benches took the place of chairs at the table. There were trunks or chests for clothing and shelves for dishes."*[37]

In *Pioneer Girl*, Laura described their claim shanty on the Ingalls homestead. It only had one room and a curtain divided off a bedroom. At night a bed was made on the floor of the main room. By day, that bed was taken up and placed on top of the bed in the bedroom. A quilt covered them both and Laura said that it then looked neat and cozy.

Some homesteaders built soddies, houses built of sod. Even though they were made of dirt, they were actually better, especially in winter, than claim shanties.

> "O.W. Coursey, who lived in a sod house near Virgil, S.D., wrote: "We cut the sod into sections 14 by 28 inches. The walls at the base were 28 inches and about three feet above the ground we began to taper the walls inward. At the top they were about 14 inches." Before lumber became plentiful, sod houses were very common. They were warm and comfortable."[38]

A claim shanty was quicker to build than a soddy, even if it wasn't as warm.

> "When railroads reached the frontier, as they did in Montana in 1880, materials such as lumber, tar paper, and shingles were immediately available to newly arrived homesteaders. The sod house was abandoned in favor of the board-and-batten claim shanty, as it was much easier for settlers to build a frame shelter than to cut sod and stack bricks.

> Many settlers draped the ceilings of their sod houses with cheesecloth or muslin to catch falling debris. Homestead shanties, like log cabins and soddies before them, were usually comprised of one (usually fairly small) room. Shanties were often built directly on the ground, with a dirt floor and no foundation. Shanty walls consisted of studs, horizontal boxing,

and a layer of tarpaper held on with lath. On the windswept prairies, ceaseless winds could literally tear the walls from a shanty; if the walls held, poorly anchored shanties toppled over and blew away. Though shanties were more pleasant quarters than soddies in many ways, they were extremely difficult to heat in the winter -- and bake-oven hot in the summer. One Montana settler reported that she could "bake bread in July by placing it next to the steaming tar-paper wall."

Shanties appealed to homesteaders because of their relative portability. When families with adult or nearly adult children made multiple claims in the same area, they would move the shanty around from claim to claim as "proving up" times drew near and visits from Land Office Inspectors became imminent. When settlers married, one homesteader often took their shanty to their spouse's claim to double the size of their home. After "proving up" time, shanties were easily expanded and improved. Many buildings that started out as claim shanties remain in use throughout the plains and prairies to this day."[39]

A family might have survived the hard winter in a soddy, but a board and tarpaper claim shanty was not a safe place to withstand Dakota blizzards. The October blizzard and the thick muskrat houses and the rushing geese caused Pa, during a nice spell of weather after the first storm, to move his family into the town of De Smet for the winter. He had built a store building in the new town and they moved in there. As one of the early settlers, Pa was a county commissioner and a Justice of the Peace. He conducted his business in the front room of the store. The family's kitchen and living space was in the room behind that. A lean-to was attached to the rear of the building and bedrooms were upstairs. Others who wintered in town lived in a similar fashion, if that may be called fashion.

When they were settled in town, Laura and Carrie were able to attend school. *The Long Winter* points out that Ma Ingalls dressed Laura warmly for school, over her itchy objections.

Good thing.

Not long after they had moved into town while Laura and Carrie were at school in their itchy long johns – another blizzard hit.

The best way to face a blizzard was not to be out in one. If a blizzard cloud loomed, everyone tried to get home before it hit.

All those kids in De Smet, however, were caught at school when the blizzard blew in. The teacher did not know whether to send the children out in the storm to go home, or keep them in the schoolhouse and try to wait out the storm there. Laura knew that the school building was a long walk from town, and in a blizzard there was no way to see the buildings in town to tell where to go. De Smet was only two blocks long. If they missed it, there was nothing beyond.

Laura remembered that there were fifteen students in the school, the sun was shining and the air was still when the blizzard hit. A townsman came to help them find their way home.

> "We started all alone together following Mr. Holms and Miss Garland, but after a few minutes Cap Garland left the others and went farther to the south. We shouted at him but he

disappeared in the storm running. We were blinded by the snow, buffeted by the wind until we could hardly keep our feet and awfully cold. It seemed to me that we had already gone too far and still there was no sign of buildings when suddenly we ran against the back of a building that stood at the very end of the street, the last building in town on the north. We didn't see it until we bumped against it and if we had gone just a few feet farther north we should have missed it and been out on the open prairie lost in the blizzard.

Cap Garland went straight, told the men down town that we had gone wrong and a crowd was just starting after us when we came walking up the street beside the buildings."[40]

Laura's teacher, who was Cap Garland's sister,[41] chose to try to get the children home rather than stay in the schoolhouse. They were almost lost in the blizzard, though, Laura said, and headed for a certain death.

Was that just hyperbole for effect? Were Laura and Carrie and the others really in that much danger?

That same year another teacher in Minnesota chose to stay with the children in a school during a blizzard, instead of trying to get home through the storm. George H. Wallace, a writer for the *Waukesha Freeman* newspaper in Waukesha, Wisconsin, wrote an account of the *Winter of the Big Snow* in 1933. More than fifty years later, he recalled one of the more grim memories of that memorable year.

"A school teacher in a sparsely settled district of Minnesota, where scholars came as far as six miles to attend school, was

frozen to death with her scholars whom she vainly endeavored to save, when their scant fuel supply was exhausted during a 40 below zero blizzard."[42]

Seven years after the hard winter, the winter of 1888 had two of the worst blizzards ever known. One was called the School Children's Blizzard or the Schoolhouse Blizzard.

In an article about the School Children's Blizzard of 1888, an Iroquois, South Dakota historical account describes the conditions at that time. Iroquois is a town only about fifteen miles west of De Smet.

"In 1888, pioneer children were mainly educated in one-room school houses. School houses were not only located in the small Dakota towns, but were also scattered throughout the countryside.

There were very few teachers in this new territory, so teachers of that time were mostly teenaged girls. These young girls could write their exam and earn their teacher's certificate by age 16. Most schools had one coal burning stove placed in the center of the room. There were no buses or cars. Children walked to school, or if they were lucky, rode a horse. Their walk to school may have been a mile or more. When blizzards came up, the young teacher had to decide if she should take the chance of keeping her students in the school and possibly run out of fuel and freeze or flee into the storm, hoping to find the shelter of the closest home.

Ray H. Miller's father was an early pioneer in Beadle County in 1882. His family of eight had a small but comfortable house on their homestead.

On January 12, 1888, the day started like any other. Large snowflakes were falling to the ground, and a slight breeze was blowing from the southwest. The morning temperatures were mild.

While watering his team of oxen, Miller's father saw a dark cloud quickly approaching from the west. The oxen, acting very uneasy, sensed something was wrong and ran to the barn.

The four oldest Miller children were in school when the storm hit. Their father started out to look for them. After walking a short distance, his face was a mask of snow and ice, and he was unable to continue. The temperature had dropped to 34 below zero and the wind was fiercely blowing at 70 miles per hour. Mr. Miller turned around and crawled back to his house.

The school house was located near the Sprague homestead and Mr. Sprague was able to lead the students through the storm to shelter.

Many people and livestock in Dakota Territory died in this storm. Ray Miller's mother called that day a nightmare. She could not forget it, or the fact that so many people died in the storm, some found only a few feet from their homes."[43]

A history of Pawnee County, Nebraska recalls the same 1888 blizzard in that state.

"On her way home from elementary school classes on Thursday afternoon, January 12, at Table Rock, Neb., 11-year-old Avis Dopp was caught in the fury of the violent winter assault. A blinding barrage of snowflakes was driven by strong

winds which wrapped schoolgirls' skirts around their legs, frightfully impairing efforts of the youngsters to reach safety. Battling the powerful force of the stiff cold air currents, and stumbling through the reduced visibility of the fierce snowy gale, young Avis "was down more than up," and her hands froze painfully during the lengthy one-block trip to her house. Flora Dopp, a former nurse, revived her suffering daughter's agonized hands in cold water, while the girl believed her fingernails were starting to come off.

The unresolved fate of absent loved ones tormented other worried residents who themselves had successfully found refuge during the widespread turmoil. At the Dopp house, the anxious females feared for Avis' father, a teacher who daily commuted on horseback to his school west of Pawnee City. Avis recalled the tremendous storm lasted from 2:00 p. m. till 6:00 p. m., leaving drifted snowbanks and frigid temperatures which made conventional travel very hazardous.

The winter sky cleared just before dusk, Avis later remembered, after three or four feet of snow had fallen and the strong winds had caused drifting. In the aftermath of the massive blizzard, Seymour H. Dopp kept his 17 pupils protected overnight in the country schoolhouse, where they had stockpiled fuel for a warm fire, and sheltered his faithful riding horse in the chilly enclosure of an unheated cob shed.

The next morning, on Friday the 13th, concerned parents of the stranded students guided horse teams over snow-covered country roads as they negotiated farm wagons through the deep drifts all the way to Seymour Dopp's schoolhouse. And once there, the relieved adults happily rescued their weary and hungry children. Astride his reliable steed, schoolmaster Dopp then successfully navigated through all the white stuff back to his own family awaiting in snowbound Table Rock."[44]

The *Encyclopedia Britannica*, 1893 edition, published only five years after the 1888 event, gives this account.

"In one [blizzard] which visited Dakota and the States of Montana, Minnesota, Nebraska, Kansas and Texas in January, 1888, the mercury fell within twenty-four hours from 74° above zero to 28° below in some places, and in Dakota went down to 40° below zero. In fine clear weather, with little or no warning, the sky darkened and the air was filled with snow, or ice-dust, as fine as flour, driven before a wind so furious and roaring that men's voices were inaudible at a distance of six feet. Men in the fields and children on their way from school died ere they could reach shelter; some of them having been not frozen, but suffocated from the impossibility of breathing the blizzard. Some 235 persons lost their lives. This was the worst storm since 1864; the Colorado River in Texas was frozen with ice a foot thick, for the first time in the memory of man."

Over a century later, the Weather Notebook noted this same blizzard in its commentary.

"The most famous blizzard in Great Plains history hit on January 12th, 1888. "It was a mild morning, and then it began snowing very heavily."

Lena Tetzlaff was twelve years old that day.

"And blowing, until it was impossible to see more than about six to ten feet ahead of you. And kept it up all day and all night."

Tetzlaff remembers the storm in the 1960 recording made when she was 85. She survived the storm in her parents' home on a farm in what is now northeastern South Dakota. She recalls that within hours, the temperature dropped from seventy-four degrees to minus forty. The storm was named the "Schoolchildren's Blizzard," because many children were caught in one-room schoolhouses, including Tetzlaff's classmates.

"Two men tied a rope to the last house and went in the direction where the schoolhouse stood. And when they got to that place they tied it to the railing and made each child take a hold of the rope and walk down to the end of the rope, where parents came and took the children on home."

Tetzlaff's seventeen-year-old cousin George was among the unlucky when he froze to death returning from town on horseback. All told, two hundred people and tens of thousands of cattle died in the blizzard that stretched from Canada to Texas, freezing the ice of the Colorado River to a foot thick. The School House Blizzard was one of the most devastating to hit the heartland, stirring sharp memories for at least one survivor, Lena Tetzlaff, even after 72 years had passed." [45]

Again, that School Children Blizzard was not during the hard winter, but it dramatically shows the real danger that Laura, Carrie and the other students were facing. Laura's story of the blizzard at school in De Smet was not just exaggeration for effect. It was very possible to be lost in a blizzard going from the schoolhouse to home and Laura and Carrie and Mary Power and Minnie Johnson and all the other kids at school, except for Cap Garland, almost were. In the blinding blizzard, they bumped into the last building in town. Had they missed it, there was nothing beyond except blinding white and freezing cold and almost certain death.

As it was, they all found their way home safely. In the warmth of Pa's building in town, Laura's eyelids bled from being beaten by the driven snow, her coat crackled with crinkles of ice and her chilled body shivered numbly, but she and Carrie and all her other schoolmates were safe at home after the blizzard at school.

~~~~~

Chapter 5

Train Trouble

Once Laura was safe back at home, the blizzard made its three day run and everyone stayed safely indoors. After the storm left, life in De Smet tried to get back to normal. Life simply could not get back to normal, though.

Why not?

It was not a normal winter.

The railroad built frontier towns along the rail line. Those towns sprang up where none had been before. Around them, farms spouted on the wild prairie, or what families hoped would be farms. Most of the new frontier farmers, like Pa Ingalls, had not been able to harvest a crop in the summer of 1880. The little towns had a few stores, but they were too new to have a big stock of goods.

That one winter, that one railroad track was the frontier towns' link to life. They expected to get their necessities by the railroad. They planned to survive the winter with the railroad. The frontier towns thought that the brand new railroad, with its miles of gleaming tracks, would surely stay open.

After all, what could stop a steam locomotive that, with its tender car of coal, weighed forty tons?

A railroad has to run fairly close to level, and little hills on the prairie were cut through to keep the track elevation constant. The blizzards had filled those cuts with frozen snow. In a few days, the railroad had the cuts open again.

But the snow kept filling them up again.

> *"Storms followed storms so quickly that the railroad track could not be kept open. The Company kept men shoveling snow and snow plows working all they could, but the snow plows stuck in the snow and snow blew back faster than the men could shovel it out."*[46]

The railroad hired the men of De Smet to do the shoveling and paid them good wages at two dollars a day. The men would likely have shoveled for nothing, though, just the keep the trains running. The more the snow came, the more they shoveled, and the higher the snow banks got on each side of the cuts. Eventually it took three men to get one shovel full of snow away from the tracks, passing the snow up from one to the other.

In *The Long Winter*, Pa and the men of De Smet helped clear the tracks after the schoolhouse blizzard, and a train did get through, but it was only a work train, carrying workers, not food or coal. Pa then told Ma and the girls the story of the train superintendent who tried to break through the snow on the tracks. In *Pioneer Girl*, Laura simply wrote that story in a straightforward manner.

> *"The superintendent of the Division was much displeased at the failure of his men to get the trains through and came out to the deep cut west of Tracy to supervise the work himself. They were using two snow plows hitched together, but the snow was*

packed so hard that they could drive them only a few feet when they stuck fast and had to be shoveled out.

The superintendent ordered them to put three plows on and drive them through. Then the engineer refused to drive the engine in front saying they would all be killed. The superintendent replied that he wouldn't ask a man to do anything he wouldn't do himself and – with an oath – he'd drive the engine himself. They put the other plow on, backed the train for a mile, then came as fast as they could and struck the snow in the cut with all the power of the engines, their weight and speed. And stopped!

The front engine and its plow were completely buried, even the smoke stack covered. By a miracle the engineers were not hurt and crawled and were shoveled out. The impact, the heat and steam from the engine in front melted the snow close around it and it froze again in solid ice.

When the men had shoveled the snow away so they could get to it they had to use picks to cut the ice from the wheels and gearing. It took two days with all the men that could work around them to get the engines loose. By that time another blizzard was raging and the Superintendent ordered all work on the track stopped with the snow one hundred feet deep on the track at the Tracy cut and twenty-five feet deep on the track in the cut just west of De Smet."[47]

Tracy, Minnesota was about a hundred miles east of De Smet. All the railroad towns on that rail line west of Tracy were snowed in, including Brookings, Volga and De Smet.

The *History of Dakota Territory* talked of the difficulty on that one rail line.

> *"The Brookings Line was in the heaviest part of the storm of October 15th, and was blocked for several weeks, in fact was hardly free from blockade until the spring following."*[48]

This detailed history mentions the notorious Tracy cut that Laura noted often in her book.

> *"[B]etween Tracy and Sleepy Eye there was one cut where the snow was sixty-five feet deep, and a number that were covered from twenty to forty feet."*[49]

In all fairness to the Chicago and Northwestern Railroad, they struggled mightily to keep their lines open. The *History of Dakota Territory* gives us more detail about that struggle.

> *"Railroad travel and traffic was interrupted by this first storm, snow plows were required to clear away the accumulations in the cuts, and thereafter snowstorms were of such frequent occurrence that there was barely a week for half a year when the roads made their schedule time, but there were many weeks when traffic and travel by rail was entirely suspended, and this was the rule throughout the region west of the Mississippi and north of the forty-second parallel of latitude.*
>
> *Dakota had been receiving many thousands of new settlers during the year and many thousands the year before who had made but scanty improvements on their claims, but sufficient for an ordinary winter. New lines of railroad had been extended across the territory in 1880, and scores of new towns founded into which thousands of people had settled and were living in cramped and exposed quarters, altogether unsuitable for any sort of comfort in winter. And the railroads had not yet shipped in the winter's supply of coal or other fuel, so that this*

essential was one of the earliest "necessities of life" that was discovered to be lacking.

Train loads of fuel were on the tracks, bound for Dakota, but snowbound and unable to move; and it was later claimed that some trains thus laden lay for months buried in drifts on side tracks, and that human power was inadequate to remove them. The ordinary autumn season would have given good weather for at least a month or six weeks longer, but this early October visitation placed an embargo on railway transportation from the start...[50]

The "many thousands of new settlers" streaming into Dakota Territory were banking on the trains to get them through the winter. They had planned to buy what they needed, and they had the money, but it never occurred to them that this modern technological marvel – the Iron Horse – might let them down.

The situation would not have been so critical if the October blizzard had not arrived so early, before merchants had laid in enough stock to last a while. When the trains couldn't run, those much needed supplies quickly ran short, including coal for heat. John Stanley, a settler in Gary, Dakota Territory pointed out how quickly the towns ran out of supplies.

"That [October] storm had blocked the only railroad in that part of Dakota, and it was the latter part of November before the tracks were cleared and a train reached town. Some necessities had become depleted-merchants not anticipating further blizzards of that type so early in the season. After about a week with regular train service another big snowstorm came, then another, and another, all winter blocking all railroad traffic for about six months, until April 1881."[51]

In fact, even the trains themselves ran out of coal to fire their steam engines. *The History of Dakota Territory* said that steam trains sometimes ran on corn. They ran on roasting ears!

However, with either coal or corn, the train could not get through the snow.

> *"... By the close of December the supply of coal throughout this western country was so nearly exhausted that corn was substituted.... It was related in one of the local papers, December 29th, that "the train started out from Sioux Falls for Sioux City with Master Mechanic Moulton aboard, and with a supply of corn for fuel, but on reaching the cuts four miles below the town it encountered a snowdrift 400 feet long which it found impossible to 'buck through,' and the effort was given up and the train returned to the falls.*
>
> *At this time the Chicago, Milwaukee & St. Paul issued a general order that for the time being, and until further notice, the running of all trains west of Mason City, Ia., was suspended."*[52]

Mason City, Iowa is just south of the Minnesota border and three hundred miles southeast of De Smet. That shows just how much of the upper Midwest was strangled by the snow.

> *"This condition existed in Minnesota, Iowa, Dakota, Nebraska, and for that matter throughout the Northwest. It was a winter unprecedented in heavy and frequent snows and cold weather. Tens of thousands of range cattle perished. After the first heavy storms the roads were cleared, but were easily blockaded by another snowfall even of moderate amount. Conditions which, in a milder manner, occur every snowy winter prevailed in an aggravated form in 1881.*

This was caused by the frequency of the storms, which filled the railway cuts and made the wagon roads almost impassable for animals.

In the railway cuts the snow would be shoveled clear of the track on each side, and frequently it occurred that the tracks were no sooner cleared, and often while the work of clearing them was in progress, another snowstorm would break loose that would cover the tracks sufficiently to stop traffic. This frequent clearing of the tracks piled the snow banks higher on each side, and it was not an unusual occurrence, later in the season, when trains began running, for the passenger to find the train plunging into what appeared to be a tunnel, the snow banks having grown to be higher than the car roofs so as to shut out the light."[53]

L. B. Albright was a minister in Pierre, which later became the capital of South Dakota, during the hard winter. Pierre had been a trading post since shortly after the Louisiana Purchase in 1803, but only became a town when the railroad reached there in 1880. It is about 150 miles west of De Smet, and although positioned on the Missouri River, the new town was in much the same situation as De Smet. They also depended on the new rail line.

Albright complained that conditions were so bad, he couldn't get people interested in going to church!

"It had been very cold, 10 degrees below zero for several days. The river was frozen over, and it was snowing almost every day. On the 20th of December the last train left Pierre and from that time until May 8th, 1881, the road was blocked from Winona, Minnesota west. In a short time after trains quit

running the town was out of coal, meat of all kinds, butter and kerosene...

The great object of every one at that time was to get a place to stay and to get something to eat . . . It was so cold and almost impossible to get fuel . . . Conditions were such that it was almost impossible to get people interested in church matters."[54]

In 1934, Albright authored a pamphlet, *A Half Century in Pierre,* and included these memories of the hard winter fifty-four years earlier.

"Everything was moving fast in Pierre. The Railroad Co. held a sale of lots in Oct. The first regular train reached Pierre on November 4th and there was a rush to get buildings up before winter stopped all work. Three hotels were under way, the Chicago & North Western and the North Western Transportation Co., were building offices and warehouses, and all kinds of business houses were being built. The block from Dakota Ave. to Missouri Ave., on Pierre St., was considered the best location for business and was covered with business houses.

Snow was falling almost every day and we heard that the road would probably be blocked. Mr. West went to Ohio to get married and got through on the last train east on December 20th, and we were snowed in until the first train came through on the 8th of May, 1881. After the trains stopped running it became very cold with deep snow and we could not do any work so put in a long and tiresome winter.

The saloons and dance halls were in full operation, the saloons had a bar on one side and gambling tables on the other. During

> the winter we received a few mails. The stage from Yankton made a few trips and a few mails were brought in from the Black Hills.
>
> The railway was completely blocked from Winona west. The Weekly Signal was our only paper but it soon stopped for lack of material. The last edition was printed on straw paper. Our chief amusement was cards.
>
> I was alone at our lumber office but lived very well as we had shipped in some supplies from Winona and Mr. West's relatives, farmers in Iowa, had sent him a box containing a generous supply of butter, bacon and other things that I appropriated. I had the only kerosene, bacon and butter in town, so was the envy of the poor fellows who did not have anything to grease their griddles."

Perhaps that also had something to do with people not showing interest in coming to his church meetings.

It's hard to imagine snow so deep that a steam locomotive can't push it aside. Those old iron horses were enormously heavy, run by tremendously powerful steam engines, yet they could not push through all that snow. Doane Robinson's *History of South Dakota* talks about those mountains of snow that trains couldn't cross.

> "The great blizzard of the middle of October, 1880, was the initial performance of a winter unprecedented, and never succeeded in severity, in the history of Dakota or the northwest. Heavy snows and severe storms came at frequent intervals, rendering train service unreliable and uncertain, hindering the removal of crops and the shipment into the country of supplies of fuel and groceries.

Early in January on many lines train service became utterly impracticable. It was before the invention of the rotary snow plow, and the constantly accumulating masses of snow blown back and forth by violent winds filled the cuts to a vast depth. More than eleven feet of snow fell during the season and all of it remained in the country, there being no thawing weather.

Hundreds of snow-shovelers were employed by the railways leading to Dakota. They would attack a drifted cut, and shovel the snow out and into great banks upon either side. The winds of that night would possibly fill the enlarged cut to the brim, and another day's work would simply result in raising the banks higher, making place for deeper drifts. In this way mountains of snow were built up over the tracks in the very places where the greatest effort was made to open them. Even in the open places it was no uncommon thing to find the telegraph wires buried under the snow."[55]

Laura remembered when the last train came through De Smet. There were about a hundred people living in town. They had two grocery stores that sold food and a lumber yard that sold coal. Those stores began with minimal stock – that's all they could afford – and expected to replace their sparse inventory as they sold it. They expected to receive shipments of food and coal all winter via the railroad.

Even in this undramatic account by Laura, you can still sense the disappointment they felt when they realized there would be no trains and no additional food for the rest of the winter.

"The storms were so terrible and so frequent that teaming from Brookings could not be done and supplies were short even there for no train could run west of Tracy and the country was all new.

> *We were wondering how we would get through the winter and were so relieved when on January 4th we heard the train whistle. Everyone ran to the depot but it was only a train carrying passengers and mail. We thought there must be another train coming behind with food and fuel but none came and that night there was the worst storm yet; the track was buried again, orders came over the telegraph wires to lay off all work and we knew we could expect no help from outside. We must depend on ourselves."*[56]

When Laura wrote about the hard winter, she had lived well on an Ozarks farm for about forty-five years. In fact, in 1917 Laura wrote that she and Almanzo had enough food and supplies to last them a whole year, without needing to buy anything at all, if they chose not to.[57] Recalling those lean times when there was not enough food to eat that terrible winter must have sobered her severely.

> *"There was no meat to be had, no butter, the potatoes were nearly gone. The only fruit there had been in town was dried fruit and that was long since gone from the stores. We had a little yet and a little bit of sugar. Coffee was gone and tea. Pa had a little wheat he had bought for seed the next spring and Ma browned that, ground it and made us a hot drink. What with the terrible cold and just dry hay to eat our cows were nearly dry. Pa got about a quart at a milking and the most of that went to Grace and Maggie on account of the baby. Our sugar was gone and the last sack at the store had sold for 50 cents a pound. Then the flour was all gone, the last sack of that sold for one dollar a pound. There was no more coal nor kerosene.*[58]

Edward Jensen, the first Norwegian settler in Grant County, South Dakota wrote that like many households, his family also ground wheat in a coffee mill.

> "[W]e had to grind our wheat in the coffee mill so we could keep ourselves in bread, porridge and soup through the winter. As to side dishes there was nothing to be said since, as mentioned, we had not shopped."[59]

Like the Ingalls, pioneers on the plains were rugged and resourceful. Robinson points out that people often lived together that winter to save resources.

> "In every town the business men organized themselves into relief committees to see that there was an equitable distribution of such supplies as could be secured, and they extended their relief work over all of the adjacent territory so that all were supplied, and, while there was great hardship, there was very little real suffering. Several families would colonize in one habitation to save fuel."[60]

One of the most depressing things about the hard winter was having to spend so much time in the dark. It could have been called the dark winter, too, although it already seems to have enough names. Winter days were short, of course, but with the frequent storms the sun often did not shine at all. Even the daylight was dark, with people cooped up in a single room with a small window and blizzards often blocking out what light there was from outside.

> "One of the great inconveniences was the lack of oil for lighting. The country was new and the production of lard and tallow only as yet

nominal. The kerosene at the stores lasted but a few days after the trains stopped, and many families were compelled for several months to sit in darkness."[61]

The *Fort Pierre Times*, in a February 17, 1937 article titled *Freighting in the 80's,* talked about the shortage of kerosene for lighting during the hard winter.

"Mason Martin, one of the original settlers living here when the town was but a scattering of log houses and when firearms and whiskey were considered articles of trade, came to South Dakota in 1880. The year of Martin's advent into Dakota territory is recalled by two events: the coldest, most prolonged siege of winter the state has experienced and the building of the Chicago and Northwestern railway into Dakota as far as Pierre.

In December of that year Martin set out for Deadwood with a load of freight, his chief cargo being about two tons of kerosene. Reaching the Cheyenne river he was informed that the merchant for whom he was freighting had offered a $50 bonus if he arrived in Deadwood with his cargo on a certain day, for the supply of illuminating fuel in the town had been depleted.

When he arrived with the much-needed source of lighting he said he never had a chance to carry his cargo into the store. Residents surrounded his wagon and bought the entire cargo of kerosene at $2 a gallon. Martin had left Pierre for Deadwood in December but it was April when he returned. The pioneer railroad fared little better, he said, Pierre not having had a train all winter."[62]

Resourcefulness peaks during times of greatest need. When

they needed light and had no kerosene for lamps, Ma Ingalls made a button light with axle grease. It only made a little light, like a candle, but it was light and did break the darkness.[63]

For heat, people in Dakota customarily burned coal shipped in on the railroad. On the prairies, there were no forests for firewood, other than by streams. People often picked up, stacked and burned buffalo chips or cow chips, which is dried manure. But there were not enough of those lying around and few had collected them. So when the settlers couldn't buy coal, they were reduced to burning hay to keep from freezing to death.

As Laura recalls, the settlers had a technique for turning loose hay into twisted sticks. She described that at length in *The Long Winter*. As you can imagine, that was no easy task.

> *"It was quite a trick to take a handful of the hay,"* Laura wrote, *"an end in each hand, twist it until it kinked on itself in the middle, then twisting the two sides, upon each other until the ends were reached, make a sort of knot and tuck the ends in to hold it tight."*[64]

That trick made a stick of hay about a foot long and a few inches around. It burned hot and quick. Somebody had to make hay sticks all day long to have enough fuel and heat to stay alive.

The Ingalls did not come up with the idea of making sticks out of tough, long prairie hay. There was, in fact, a prairie song that mentioned burning twisted hay.

My Old Sod Shanty on My Claim

I am looking rather seedy now
While holding down my claim
And my vittles are not always served the best
And the mice play slyly around me
As I lay me down to sleep
In my little old sod shanty on my claim.

Chorus:

Oh the hinges are of leather
And the windows have no glass
Round my little old sod shanty on my claim.

Oh, when I left my eastern home,
So happy and so gay
To try to win my way to wealth and fame
I little thought that I would come
To burning twisted hay
In my little old sod shanty on my claim.[65]

Twisting hay to burn as fuel was not uncommon among the first settlers. A North Dakota settler typified that song.

> *"Herman began to work the homestead adjoining that of his brother's land by the spring of 1880. Like thousands of other settlers on the plains, he began his new life by building a sod hut. Within a few months of their arrival in Cass County, the Boehm brothers' were given a welcome to Dakota Territory for which they and most other newly arrived settlers were completely unprepared. It came in the form of an early*

blizzard, beginning on October 15 a heavy, dense snow began to fall. And as most people had not stored fuel or food, they were forced to burn corn and hay in their stoves."[66]

Beatrice Wade Sipher and her family lived about ten miles northwest of De Smet, as pointed out earlier. In her journal, she also mentions burning hay for fuel in the winter.

"We used to burn twisted slough hay, and cooked and kept warm in winter with that kind of fuel. Later we burned "chips" or "oxoline." It was better than nothing and made a good fire. Some folks had straw burners, but we never used one. They used to puff and fill the house with smoke."[67]

Chips, of course, were dried cow, ox or buffalo manure – oxoline! The following people would have rejoiced to have had a supply of oxoline.

On March 15, 1881, the *New York Times* reported from Chicago that in the northwestern part of the state of Illinois ...

"there is a vast amount of suffering among the people caused by the snow blockages and the impossibility of getting provisions and fuel. In O'Brien County, four families took shelter in one house and used the other three houses for fuel. The snow averages four feet in depth, and is badly drifted."[68]

So when the trains quit running, the settlers were hurting for food, fuel and light. John Stanley of Gary, South Dakota remembered what it was like to be six months without the train.

"It proved to be a winter of successive blizzards, snow storms and wind, but with many bright sunny days-and shut off from

> the outside world way out there in that sparsely settled prairie region of Dakota. With those long six months without train service and with no additions to the mercantile supplies to the stores, practically all staple necessities gave out-including flour, meat, sugar, kerosene, etc."[69]

Under more normal conditions frontier farmers hunted to supplement their food supply, but not that winter, John said.

> "The trials and hardships that were endured by many all over that vast region in Western Minnesota and eastern Dakota was a history-making epoch-though not recorded and therefore now practically unheard of. All wild animal life had either made its way out to where better conditions prevailed or had starved to death-becoming extinct. There were no wild-game animals left to provide meat."

He points out that settlers around Gary were better off than those around De Smet, because they did have a supply of wheat.

> "After all supplies of flour were exhausted everyone resorted to coffee mills and ground their own whole-wheat flour. Most farmers fortunately had plenty of grain stored away, for winter had come before they had marketed all their crops. This coffee-mill grinding process kept some member of the family busy a good part of the time, and I would like to pay my respects to the value and popularity of the whole wheat products of those days-bread, muffins, pancakes, etc. The coffee mill was worn out, and now in later years we regret it was not saved as a souvenir."

With unending cold and sparse provisions, you would think that illness would have been widespread that winter. According to Mr. Stanley, though, the opposite was true.

> *"Those who chanced to have vegetables, a few pigs and possibly their own beef considered they lived high and handsomely. The situation was met without much complaint, and after it was over and with no loss of life, all seemed to think they had enjoyed the new experience, for they kept in perfect health, and were largely occupied trying to provide themselves with food stuffs and fuel, while those who had plenty of books and magazines were indeed lucky. The local weekly newspaper finally exhausted its print paper as well as the town's supply of wallpaper. Many families had to twist hay and straw into compact "sticks" for fuel..."* [70]

Peter Philp emigrated from Scotland to America in 1880. That August he arrived in Codington County, South Dakota. His timing was not the best.

> *"Peter Philp was born in Thronton, Fifeshire, Scotland, on August 27, 1838. After securing a good education in the schools of his native land he learned the trade of iron moulding and followed the same in various parts of Scotland until about 1875 or 1876, from which time until his removal to America, in 1880, he followed agricultural pursuits. June 19, 1866, he contracted a matrimonial alliance with Elizabeth Anderson, of Fifeshire, daughter of Robert and Margaret (seas) Anderson, and in 1880, as stated above, he brought his family to America, making his way direct to Codington county, South Dakota, and entering several hundred acres of land in what is now the township of Waverly."*

Waverly is about sixty miles northeast of De Smet, near Watertown. As Peter arrived there right before winter, he tried to prepare for it.

> "Mr. Philp reached his new home in August of the above year and during the ensuing fall he put up a house and as best he could prepared for the winter that was soon to follow. The winter of 1880-81 is remembered as the most severe ever known and the vicissitudes, hardships and sufferings of the settlers during that season of awful cold, piercing winds and frightful blizzards, cannot be described by either tongue or pen."

Soon he was forced to do like so many other setters, including the Ingalls – spend all day grinding wheat and twisting hay, every day, all winter.

> "Mr. Philp's stock of provisions was exhausted long before the terrible winter ended. And for weeks at a time the only food of the family consisted of wheat ground to the consistency of course flour in a coffee-mill. To keep from freezing after their fuel was gone, they had recourse to hay, and to make this last as long as possible, only small quantities were burned at a time, the members of the family huddling closely around the fire so as to utilize every particle of the precious heat."[71]

So the settlers in De Smet and many other towns across the Great Plains sat in the dark, huddled around their little fires of dried grass, and ground wheat grain by grain in little coffee mills. Still the snow came. As the winter wore on and the people wore out, the blizzards did not.

In Wisconsin, the Waukesha newspaper recalled the ongoing winter storms.

"During the last few days of January, 1881, there were severe rain and sleet storms, followed by severe snows almost continuously until the night of Feb. 1. The word blizzard was then just coming into common use and this series of storms established it for all time, for it was a real blizzard."[72]

Settlers often had livestock to tend during the winter. The deep snow made normal chores a lot more difficult, and very unusual at times. Robinson talks about having to dig a well in the snow to tend his animals.

"On the 2d of February, when it appeared that nature had exhausted all of her resources in supplying material for drifts, a snow storm set in which continued without cessation for nine days. In the towns the streets were filled with solid drifts to the tops of the buildings and tunneling was resorted to to secure passage about town. Farmers found their homes and their barns completely covered and were compelled to tunnel down to reach and feed their stock. Among the homesteaders, "straw barns" were very popular, affording a cheap and comfortable protection for stock and these became hidden under the general level of the snow on the prairies and a favorite method of reaching stock stabled in this way was through a well sunk directly down from above, through which provender was carried in."[73]

John Stanley also mentioned digging down to the animals.

"One of the daily chores first thing each morning, was shoveling the drifted five or six feet of snow out of the entrance to the stable-which was completely covered. The entrance was made by digging a "stairway" down to the stable door, the snow becoming so hard that the horses and cattle could walk

up and down the snow steps when taken out to water, and they did it like circus-performing animals.

Added snow came occasionally-from a few inches to a couple of feet at a time. All gulches and low places were finally filled, making the whole area a vast apparently level plane-whereas that "coteaux" region was rough, with some gulches 30 to 50 feet deep."[74]

Edward Jensen, a transplant from Norway and surely no stranger to snow, commented on the depth of the white stuff.

"Our house was snowed in, so that when I had to go out to tend the livestock, I had to shovel the snow into the house to make a hole so I could get out. One should understand also that it snowed and drifted all the time. That way, I cursed one day and was blockaded the next. The haybarn and stable was also snowed in. I had enough to do from morning to night to keep alive."[75]

During that winter, the snow fell in October, November, December and January. And then in February –

it snowed.

"One of the most severe of the winter storms came on the 7th of February, 1881, and continued thirty-six hours and in some sections forty-eight hours. It embraced the entire territory..."[76]

Then from the February 11, 1881, *News Messenger* in Marshall, Minnesota, which was about twenty miles north of the infamous Tracy cut, we read:

"High winds typical storms. From Thursday night of last week (Feb. 3) until Monday morning of this (Feb. 7), this locality was visited by the heaviest and worst snow storm the oldest inhabitant, much as he hates to admit it, ever saw here. On this occasion we had both snow and wind in uncommon quantities. Instead of coming from the northwest, as most of our winter storms do, this one came from the southeast. While not very cold for a winter storm, the severe wind and drifting snow made it impossible most of the time to do anything out of door, and nearly all business was at a standstill. When it cleared off the roads were in the worst possible condition. Drifts on top of drifts so perfectly impeded travel that during Monday very few teams ventured out, although the snow was soft and melting."

In *The Long Winter*, Laura wrote that when Pa hauled hay in from the homestead into town the snow was so deep he couldn't tell where the road was. Once he left the town with the two story false fronts of the buildings sticking up, everything looked the same. He saw no fences, no trees, no lake – just the endless sameness of snow.

The Waukesha newspaper talked about buried fruit trees.

"At one time Pewaukee was cut off from the world running on to nearly two weeks, except by wire and snowshoes. New Berlin reported Feb. 24, that there was eleven feet of snow on the level in the open fields, and fruit trees were buried in it well up towards the tops."[77]

When the Ingalls lived in town that winter, they had a stable not far from the back of Pa's store building where they lived. Yet just getting from the back door to the stable was a challenge. In *Pioneer Girl*, Laura recalled how Pa tunneled between the house and the stable and was glad for the opportunity to do so; and *The Long Winter* showed Pa rejoicing over his tunnel in the deep snow. That tunnel let him do his chores in greater comfort – or at least less misery – because the wind was blocked out. Even the house was warmer inside because the snow covered the first story.

Mrs. J. D. Warden, of Wisconsin, also talked about snow tunneling in 1881.

> *"On my father's farm, 5 miles north of Chilton, we lived in a log house. We had to dig a tunnel from our house to the front gate through the drifted snow, which went far above a grown person's head, in order to get out. The roads were shoveled open where that was possible but in many places after the snow hardened, farmers drove on the snow over the top of the old high log fences and cut across the fields to avoid bad places in the road."*[78]

Although Pa rejoiced over his snow tunnel, when he had one, he was surely worried over not having enough food. The *History of Dakota Territory* was published in 1915, thirty-five years after the hard winter and twenty-five years before *The Long Winter* was published, and that history confirms the conditions in De Smet, which the author calls "pitiable."

> *"On the eastern end of the line a pitiable condition existed. At DeSmet the people were living on flour and potatoes, with nothing but hay for fuel."*[79]

In *The Long Winter*, Laura included the suspenseful story of Almanzo Wilder and Cap Garland sledding over the prairie for twenty miles to buy wheat from a homesteader. By venturing so far away from home, Almanzo and Cap might have been caught in another blizzard. Laura said they were risking their lives.

Were conditions really that dangerous?

These fellows undoubtedly thought so.

> *"A working party composed of 100 men left Huron for Pierre about March 1st, for the purpose of shoveling out the filled up cuts which had defied the efforts of snow plows, and had blockaded the road for weeks. The party was thoroughly equipped including explosives, to succeed with the task before it.*
>
> *The men dug their way through about one-half the distance to Pierre, and were then overtaken by storms and severe cold weather. There were no towns or relief stations on the line, and no settlers. The party ran out of provisions and the entire gang was reduced to one biscuit a day to each man.*
>
> *A rescuing party was then sent out from Huron and found the men in a perilous situation, but they succeeded in getting them back to Huron alive. Many of them had their feet and hands frozen to such an extent that amputation became necessary. It was then estimated that there was over two foot of snow covering the prairies of Dakota, all packed and solidified by occasional thaws followed by freezing."*[80]

Such a trip was truly dangerous. When Almanzo made it back, his feet were cold and painful, but the pain was a good sign, because it meant he still had circulation in them and they did not have to be cut off. However, it was little wonder that Almanzo never liked cold weather.

Some question whether or not this trip actually occurred, wondering if the story was just manufactured to add suspense to the book. In *The Long Winter*, the distance was said to be twenty miles. In the original *Pioneer Girl* manuscript, the distance was twelve miles.

> *"Living twelve miles southeast was a farmer who had raised some wheat the year before and if we were all to live until spring someone must go after it. A merchant named Loftus said he would furnish the money to buy it and sell it out to the people as they needed it. It was dangerous to go after it and no one wanted to go, but finally the youngest Wilder boy and Cap Garland each with one horse, on a sled used to haul hay from the slough, started.*
>
> *I think no one really expected them to get back, for twelve miles, a good part of it through slough where the horses would break through and have to be dug out, looked almost hopeless of being done in one day and it must be done between the storms.*
>
> *It was a clear, still cold day and helping the horses through the drifts as Pa did, they made the trip safely, getting back some time after dark. A blizzard struck again before morning. The boys had charged nothing for making the trip at the peril of their lives but had cheerfully gone for the sake of the community."*[81]

Notice the detail that Laura included in her brief account of that trip. She named the two young men, the fact that they only used one horse each, the sleds they used, what kind of day it was and the trouble they had getting through the snow.

Someone later calculated that a twelve-mile trip was about all that was possible given the time frame, and indeed that is what Laura said in *Pioneer Girl*. Even the location of that homesteader is thought to be known.

Laura wrote the following article, published in the *Missouri Ruralist* on February 5, 1917. That was over twenty years before she wrote *The Long Winter*, and was probably written before she had even thought of writing a book about that one year. In this article, she also talks about two young men who made that trip, and the distance was fifteen miles.

> *"De Smet was built as the railroad went thru, out in the midst of the great Dakota prairies far ahead of the farming settlements, and this first winter of its existence it was isolated from the rest of the world from December 1 until May 10 by the fearful blizzards that piled the snow 40 feet deep on the railroad tracks. The trains could not get thru. It was at the risk of life that anyone went even a mile from shelter, for the storms came up so quickly and were so fierce it was literally impossible to see the hand before the face and men have frozen to death within a few feet of shelter because they did not know they were near safety.*
>
> *The small supply of provisions in town soon gave out. The last sack of flour sold for $50 and the last of the sugar at $1 a pound. There was some wheat on hand, brought in the fall before for seed in the spring, and two young men dared to drive 15 miles to where a solitary settler had also laid in his supply of seed wheat. They brought it in on sleds. There were no mills in town or country so this wheat was all ground in the homes in coffee mills. Everybody ground wheat, even the children taking their turns, and the resultant whole wheat flour made good bread. It was also a healthful food and there was not a case of sickness in town that winter.*

It may be that the generous supply of fresh air had something to do with the general good health. Air is certainly fresh when the thermometer registers all the way from 15 to 40 degrees below zero with the wind moving at blizzard speed. In the main street of the town, snow drifts in one night were piled as high as the second stories of the houses and packed hard enough to drive over and the next night the wind might sweep the spot bare. As the houses were new and unfinished so that the snow would blow in and drift across us as we slept, fresh air was not a luxury. The houses were not overheated in daytime either, for the fuel gave out early in the winter and all there was left with which to cook and keep warm was the long prairie hay. A handful of hay was twisted into a rope, then doubled and allowed to twist back on itself and the two ends tied together in a knot, making what we called "a stick of hay."

It was a busy job to keep a supply of these "sticks" ahead of a hungry stove when the storm winds were blowing, but every one took his turn good naturedly. There is something in living close to the great elemental forces of nature that causes people to rise above small annoyances and discomforts."[82]

Was Laura accurate in her description of the long, hard winter?

The trains did stop running, as Laura said. Not only was De Smet cut off, but a number of other new little towns were in the same fix. As she said, people ground wheat in coffee mills, burned hay for heat, and dug tunnels to get to their stock. And as she said, Almanzo and Cap did find the settler with the wheat and make it back to town. As she described, De Smet was in a pitiable condition. Laura's description was accurate.

When spring came, it did not come. As the sun headed back into the northern hemisphere, and when the spring winds should have been blowing in from the south, more blizzards blew in from the northwest. It was just that kind of year.

~~~~~

Chapter 6

Spring?

> *"In the Spring a fuller crimson*
> *comes upon the robin's breast;*
> *In the Spring the wanton lapwing*
> *gets himself another crest;*
> *In the Spring a livelier iris*
> *changes on the burnish'd dove;*
> *In the Spring a young man's fancy*
> *lightly turns to thoughts of love."*[83]

That is true in a normal spring. However, in the little towns on the prairie in March of 1881, the robin was starving, the iris was stuck under the ice, and the young men were thinking about food, not love.

> *"January went by and February with my 15th birthday,"* Laura wrote in *Pioneer Girl*. *"March was stormy still and we began to wonder if spring would ever come. It seemed as though we had been grinding wheat and twisting hay for years."*

Of course, those storms were not just Dakota storms. Other states including Nebraska, Iowa, Minnesota and Wisconsin were also blasted by repeated blizzards.

Waukesha, Wisconsin is just west of Milwaukee. In early March, when a storm hit that area, a train en route between

Milwaukee and Waukesha got stuck in the snow. You expect automobiles to get stuck in the snow. You do not expect a train to get stuck in the snow. What do you do then? Get out and push?

The train from Milwaukee to Waukesha got stuck in the snow and couldn't go on and couldn't go back. Just stuck. The conductor, Cal Barnard, kept an hour by hour record of his experience on that snowed-in train. On March 10, he sent a letter to the *Waukesha Freeman* newspaper, which included his notes made during the storm earlier in the month.

He began his notes by simply mentioning the wind at 3:00 a.m.

> *"Snow Drift Station, 1 ¼ miles west of Wauwatosa, Mar. 3, 1881.*
>
> *3:00 a.m. – Howling."*

An hour later he expanded his description of the wind and snow.

> *"4:00 – Blizzard. New word just coming into use."*

The next hour he noted that the brakes were set, which means somebody had gotten out in that terrible storm and physically set those brakes.

> *"5:00 – More blizzard. Brakes all set to hold us in position."*

After listening to the storm blow fiercely for several hours, the conductor was even more impressed with the storm and repeated the new word for it.

"6:00 – Superlative blizzard."

An hour later he simply said,

"7:00 – More of it."

At 8:00 a.m., they had breakfast. You will notice that Mr. Barnard was obviously a Bible student.

"8:00 – Secured a loaf of bread, a cake and a gallon of milk from a Mrs. Moore at farm, quarter of a mile from track, which was first meal in 24 hours for six ladies, one baby, and 15 men. And there were no five loaves and two fishes left over either.

8:00 – Also. Sent out two spies to east to reconnoiter. (Like the spies of old in the promised land.)"

And an hour later they had their coffee. Black.

"9:00 – Passenger C. C. Olin had a package of coffee bought in Milwaukee and he braved the storm to a farm house for hot water and made 'coffee'. No sugar, cream or milk."

The next several hours they spent having lunch and then heading back where they came from.

"10:15 – Storm still raging. Scouts just returned. They brought not the Biblical bunch of grapes, but three locomotives and 40 shovelers which soon arrived.

11:15 – Kirk Dousman and George Rogers living ¼ mile from track came over with provisions for the trains.

11:15 – Train bucked its way through from the east till it met ours, when we coupled together and after shoveling our train out, we all headed back to Milwaukee, where we arrived at 12:45 p.m., where passengers slept in old depot till Sunday night when train left for Waukesha at 4:00 p.m. Snow letting up some. In cut east of Brookfield Jct., snow up to top of coaches, and arrived in Waukesha late at night."[84]

This was March, near the time of the vernal equinox, but the same newspaper reported two more blizzards soon after.

"On March 19 the worst storm of the winter begun, and the entire state was tied up. Snowplows which had heretofore served the railroads after a fashion were now useless with the small locomotives then in use, and the rotary plow was in its infancy, but one having been built. Thus, everything had to be shoveled out anew.

This storm had not been cleared up to any great extent when another came down out of the north and the country was at a standstill again."[85]

Nearby, the *Milwaukee Journal* recalled that same period.

"The wintry fall was followed by a severe winter which culminated in the historical blizzard which began the night of Mar. 2, 1881, and continued with unabated fury for three days and two nights...

Cities were smothered in huge drifts which blockaded the streets and brought industry and traffic to a standstill. Rural communities were literally buried to their roofs. Farmers on farms surrounding Milwaukee relate how they tunneled to the barns and melted the snow dug from the tunnels in tubs for water to give to the cattle. They also tell how lamps and lanterns had to be used in downstairs rooms all day long because the windows were covered with snow.

The houses became veritable refrigerators. Roaring fires had to be kept burning. Wood stores were exhausted and many farmers dug down to their rail fences for an additional supply of fuel.

...The snow stayed despite warm weather. A hard crust several feet thick resulted from the melting of the surface snow and the freezing of the water as it seeped through lower layers. The crust became so hard that it easily held the weight of a team of horses and a sled. A new system of roads over fields and fences, and in some places over the tops of trees, was formed. The entire topography of the countryside was changed. Valleys were filled level and mountainous drifts formed new hills."[86]

There were unique problems associated with frequent blizzards. For instance, the snow was so deep that it blocked the windows, so that both night and day the buildings were dark. The Ingalls store building that they lived in during the hard winter was two-story. In *The Long Winter*, Laura told of seeing the horses go by on the street, level with her eyes as she looked out from the second story.

Merchants wanted light in their stores so they could do business, although not a lot of business went on then, except perhaps in the saloons. So what did they do when the snow blocked their windows?

"Many merchants were required to dig down to permit daylight to enter the windows, for the electric light was yet to

come. Saloons were well supplied with excavators, since they paid liberally in "merchandise,' and were perhaps better off than most merchants regarding accessibility."[87]

And there was another difficulty with the big snow. How do you dig a grave when you can't find the ground?

"Disposing of the dead was a problem and even when the roads were temporarily passable, excavating in the cemetery was a huge undertaking. Possibly ere the grave would be prepared another storm would upset all plans.

Remains of loved ones were not infrequently kept in storage in the granary, or even buried temporarily in snow banks till a favorable opportunity arrived for a funeral. The writer attended a funeral April 21, 1881, when it was necessary to shovel roads nearly a mile, and then the cortege took to the fields, and finally entered the cemetery from the rear over the top of the fence."[88]

Laura said in *The Long Winter* that the storms and cold lasted through March into April. Spring had officially begun. But the days were still dark and cold, and the settlers still ground wheat and twisted hay sticks.

Would the long, hard winter ever end?

"For everything there is a season, and a time for every purpose under heaven."[89]

The winter began too early and stayed too late, but the sun was in the northern latitude, the days outlasted the nights, and the winter was out of season.

Finally one night the wind changed direction, as Laura wrote in *The Long Winter*. The northwest wind that brought snowstorms stopped, and the southern Chinook wind began. It was still wind, but a warm wind instead of a blizzard wind. And on the ninth of May, a train got through.

However, that first train was filled with –

farm equipment!

How did that happen?

Everybody knew that the towns along the line had been without provisions for most of the winter and were in great need. After going hungry for several months, they did not need farm equipment to grow food. They needed food itself.

The people were sure that the first train would bring food for their bellies. When the railroad sent a train full of equipment, the people had had a bellyful of the railroad. They were hungry and aggravated that the trains had not been able to run all winter and when the train showed up with farm equipment instead of food the men were about to wreck the train just for spite.

However, they did find some food.

Attached to the end of the train was an immigrant car; that is, a car loaded with a new settler's supplies. A settler loaded everything he had into a rail car and the train hauled it to his new hometown. In that car was his furniture, his tools, his food supplies – his life.

Immigrant cars were common. With thousands of new settlers moving into the prairies, that was the easiest way to move your stuff out west. The *Early History of Brown County*, South Dakota talked about families arriving with their immigrant cars.

> *"The families that came to Putney Township in the spring of 1880 came to Watertown in a box car, along with their furniture, livestock, and food which included evaporated milk, flour, coffee, tea, dried fruit and vegetables. Most of the livestock brought here from the Eastern States perished during the severe winter of 1880-81."*[90]

John Stanley and his brother rode along in their family's immigrant car to prevent it from being looted. They also must have taken a chamber pot with them.

> *"Therefore on a September evening in 1878 mother with five daughters, (including the baby Mayme, added to the family that year), took the west-bound passenger train, while brother Will and I (each in our teens, but I four years the older), took charge of the immigrant car that our Uncle Dave Aiken had supervised in loading with our belongings (household goods, some lumber, two horses, a cow, and various necessities for establishing a home in the western frontier country).*
>
> *The car was packed full, as we boys realized before completing that three or four days' trip. Our bed, consisted of springs and mattress with plenty of bedding, had been made on top of some lumber piled near the freight car door. Here we would have a good view of the country as the train chugged slowly along."*

They had a bed made on a stack of lumber in the railroad car, but the adventure was too great for two boys to sleep.

"Close to the foot of our bed was a barrel of water for stock; just above the barrel a nail driven into the side of the car held a lantern. The start was made after darkness had come, the lantern had been lighted, nobody evidently thinking of fastening it so that the bumping of the car might not jar the lantern off its hook. The result may be anticipated. Will and I were sitting on the bed waiting for the approaching freight train to which our car was to be attached. The abrupt crash finally came and behold we were in total darkness.

The splashed water from the barrel informed us what had happened. I managed to fish the lantern out of the barrel of water, but we had no lighted car that night. Fortunately the water was not contaminated enough to spoil it for the stock. That rather rough start, together with the new experience of traveling - the rumbling, banging freight train, a thunder and lightning storm giving us an occasional flash view of the Mississippi river as we passed along close to its banks - all was sufficient to prevent any drowsiness to come to the two boys who had never been away from home or the care of their parents. Daylight was never more welcome, somewhat west of Winona, Minnesota."[91]

That was an immigrant car, like the one that rolled into starving De Smet.

John Stanley also reported that when the trains finally made it through to Gary, South Dakota after the hard winter, the railroad again did not first send in a trainload of food. Obviously the men who ran the railroad had been well fed all winter!

"The latter part of April word was received that a train would arrive from the east on a certain day. It promised to be a scene similar to the arrival of a circus for the children. Old and young gathered at the station out of curiosity to again see a moving train - one which was hoped might bring needed supplies. Snow plows, pushed by a couple of large engines, had gone over the track to throw out the drifts, which still remained in the cuts-and that was no small affair, for those five or six months of solid drifts, hardened by winds, and with thawing and freezing, now softened somewhat by warm sunshine and spring winds, required the power of those two engines at full speed to clear the track.

Then followed the first long train, consisting mostly of immigrant cars, greatly to the disappointment of the people who had expected the arrival of a train with all sorts of foodstuffs. Father seemed to quickly observe the situation and went alongside the train after it came to a stop-and I trailed with him. However, those immigrant cars were mostly filled with household goods, machinery, a team or two, and sufficient necessaries of life to last a few months. Father conversed with some of those and finally prevailed upon one to sell him a sack of white flour, a ham, coffee and a few other provisions such as we had not seen for months. They were now real luxuries. What a feast we had that evening-hot biscuit, butter, ham, potatoes and real coffee."[92]

Back in De Smet, when the first train arrived with equipment and an immigrant car, the men physically broke into some unknown immigrant's supplies and divided the food among the famished families. That immigrant had been most careful in his provisioning, for there was a good supply of food in his car, including sugar, flour, meat, dried fruit and tea. Plus there were potatoes and wheat that he had planned to plant. Whoever the unlucky emigrant was, he was also greatly set back by the hard winter, when the hungry town took his supplies.

How about the next train that came in?

It was loaded with telegraph poles. All without salt!

C.H. Manchester and sons filed a homestead claim in early 1880, about three miles west of De Smet. A new little railroad town formed nearby, named Manchester. Laura's sister Grace lived there for much of her life and blind sister Mary lived there with Grace for a while. In the spring of 1881, some new settlers heading for Manchester were on one of those first trains into De Smet after the hard winter.

> "In 1880, the railroad had reached Manchester, bringing trade, communication, transportation, and many new settlers.
>
> William and Charles Anderson brought their families to homestead north of Manchester in 1880. They stayed on their claims that first year and had to endure many hardships during the long winter.
>
> Other early pioneers, Nathan and Benjamin Dow (Nathan Dow, also known as Nate, later married Grace Ingalls), William Dunn, and Ain Bump, filed their claims south of Manchester early in November in 1880 and then returned east. When spring finally arrived in 1881, they took the second train west. The tracks had been blocked with snow most of the winter, not being able to get supplies to the early settlements.

> *When their train stopped in DeSmet, they recalled seeing a large crowd of hungry people hoping for food supplies and wanting something to eat."*[93]

Eventually the little town of Manchester lost most of its population, losing people to Huron on the west or De Smet on the east. In 2003, a tornado destroyed what was left of the town.

Finally, the third train into De Smet arrived, carrying food. With their bellies full and the weather warming, after seven months of staying inside, people got out and did things. The long, hard winter was over.

A history of the town of Iroquois mentions that at the end of the winter, the trains had to tread lightly to keep their tracks from falling through the soft ground.

> *"When the snow began to melt, the trains traveled slowly along the tracks. The thawing ground under the tracks was sometimes soft, creating weak areas in the tracks. Alternative track needed to be built around newly formed lakes, and sloughs. Spring finally came as the last snowstorm ended May 5. The pioneers had new struggles in dealing with the flood waters of the melting snow."*[94]

With the thaw, the Big Slough near the Ingalls' farm became part of Silver Lake and other low places became big sloughs. Pa had to drive extra miles to get around all the water just to go to his homestead.

> *"Shortly after the big snow of February,"* states the *History of South Dakota*, *"a thaw came of sufficient power to soften the surface of the drifts and an immediate freeze followed forming*

an impenetrable crust and thereafter sleighing was superb. This condition continued until the 26th of April. Up to this time it seemed as if the spring sun made no impression whatever, but upon the day mentioned the break came and in twenty-four hours the snow was resolved into water and the prairies became one vast lake."[95]

For most of the people on the prairie, the flooded plains were no more than a soft, mushy end to the hard, bitter winter. The miles of endless snow turned into miles of squishy mud. More importantly, the fields could not be planted until the ground dried up.

But for those settlers who lived by the rivers, or anywhere near the rivers, or in the low plains miles from the rivers, the hard winter had one last terrible blow.

Chapter 7

The Thaw

When warm weather finally broke, an extraordinary winter's worth of frozen precipitation began to thaw and flow.

The Missouri River is the border between South Dakota and Nebraska. By the end of the winter, it was frozen into a layer of ice several feet thick. Water from the melting snows poured into that frozen river, making a flowing river of water on top of a frozen river.

> *"The early floods came before the ice in the Missouri River gave way. They were caused by the partial melting of a portion of the surface snows in the Missouri Valley, including the mountain or Black Hills tributaries. These tributaries poured immense volumes of water on to the icy surface of the Missouri before there were any substantial indications of a break-up... This phenomenon was observable in all the stream, and the extraordinary thickness and strength of the ice enabled it to resist the weight of water passing over it for a week or more. The surface of the rivers was also the bed of a heavy coating of snow that had accumulated during the winter."*[96]

Then the river ice under the flowing water also began to melt. Huge chunks of ice several feet thick broke loose, then tangled together into impromptu dams and instant lakes.

Vermillion, South Dakota lay below the bluffs of the Missouri River. Since the town's founding in 1859, they had seen floods but nothing that had threatened the town's existence. The *Dakota Republican,* published in Vermillion, calmly noted in its March 24, 1881 edition that the Missouri River had risen six feet, but was not at flood stage.

A few days later the office of the *Dakota Republican* calmly floated down the Missouri River.[97]

George Kingsbury gives a detailed account of the thaw of 1881 that devastated the town.

> *"On March 28th an ice gorge formed below Vermillion, and the water rose rapidly and began to flood the city before nightfall. The entire town was flooded in less than an hour. The people fled to the highland, leaving their homes and business places. Great damage was done to household goods and goods in the stores. The water rose to about four feet on the 28th, and remained stationary for some time.*
>
> *… At Vermillion the destruction was most complete. The city contained a population of six or seven hundred, and about one hundred and fifty dwellings, hotels, churches, banks and business houses. The town had been built on rather a narrow strip of the Missouri bottom land, just under the highland where the present substantial city is established.*
>
> *The flood with its moving ice attacked the city about midnight of March 27th. A grove of trees west of the city obstructed the ice for a time. The people were awakened by the alarm rung out by the bell of the Baptist Church, and not many minutes later the streets were thronged with many women and children, who had been hurriedly clad, all making their way to the road*

leading up the hill to the highland, some leading horses or driving cattle, with their arms full of clothing picked up in haste as best they could when leaving their homes. The alarm bell had been the agreed signal of imminent flood danger. Many of these refugees were unable to get ahead of the invading water and ice, and were compelled to wade through three feet of icy water in the darkness of midnight to reach the bluff road.

… On the 31st the water had reached nearly to the roof of many of the smaller structures, and in the morning they began to float off their foundations. The growing trees on the west had kept the ice, in large part, from entering the town up to this time. During the 31st of March and following night forty structures floated away and dashed against the ice packs lower down the valley…

For six days following, the flood remained intact, raising and lowering alternately as the gorged ice below, extending now from two to ten miles in an icy sea, clogged up and then affording a temporary opening for a brief time, only to be again dammed up by the gorging ice floe…"[98]

And then, when it seemed that things were at their worst and couldn't possibly get any worse, the flood that was caused by a winter's worth of blizzards was accompanied by –

Another blizzard.

"On the 6th of April the water again rose rapidly, the ice entered the desolate town, which yet contained a hundred or more of its best buildings; the Baptist bell again rang out its ominous and frightful clangor announcing new danger, and just about midday the

> *procession of the buildings started – some steadily and majestically facing their fate, others tottering, partly tipped over, and in the course of a couple of hours fifty-six building were floated off or wrecked near their foundations... Twenty buildings in stately processions, like swans, were observed floating off in one fleet...*
>
> *There was one night during this long peril when a blizzard prevailed, making it impossible to row a boat or remain long exposed to the freezing blast... The weather was uniformly uncomfortably cold all through the weeks of the flood."*[99]

Three-quarters of the buildings in Vermillion were destroyed, and as the article points out, twenty buildings floated off at one time, like a fleet of ships. After the flood of 1881, the town of Vermillion moved up to the bluffs overlooking the river. Perhaps out of sympathy, the Missouri River also moved and cut a new channel about three miles away from town.[100]

Imagine the mental state of settlers who went through the rigors of staking out a claim, building a house, breaking the root tangled sod, enduring the long, hard winter, and then suffered the terrifying experience of floating down the Missouri River –

in their houses.

That happened to the Hansons, who lived in the bottoms between Yankton and Vermillion.

> *"These people were at Hans J. Hanson's house, about ten miles above Vermillion, and had procured a skiff in which they were seated, when the house, with ten people in it, was lifted from its foundation and floated away.*

> *The occupants of the house were Hans J. Hanson, O. J. Hanson, their wives and children. After the house got started on its voyage the men folks, realizing their peril, made their way to the roof, where they built a large box to serve as a life boat in case of further emergency. The house moved along, but had settled nearly to the eaves when the life boat was finished and the ten passengers found places in it; and then, with much paddling, the passengers made their way to solid ground."*[101]

With their *"much paddling,"* they made it to high ground. Needless to say, the high spots in the flooded bottoms became crowded.

> *"Gunderson's mill, seven miles west of Vermillion, was a type of an isolated settlement. As late as the 25th of April parties had been unable to make their way to it owing to the heavy ice that obstructed every avenue; cakes of ice that stood up in great sheets ten or fifteen feet in height.*
>
> *This mill was built on one of the highest points on the Missouri bottom, and was regarded as "floodproof." Near by on the same eminence were two farm houses, those of Thomas Thompson and Mr. Johnson. At the mill during the flood there were forty-two people, thirty-six in Thompson's house and forty-seven at Johnson's – 125 in all...They had been living for some time on flour only, with a very light diet of everything eatable that could be scraped up in the buildings they inhabited."*[102]

Of course, the livestock in the area that had survived the hard winter were in grave peril. Farmers could not drive their cattle to dry land, because dry land might not be anywhere near.

> *"Tens of thousands of domestic animals were swallowed up in the icy waters... The inundation had been so overwhelming and its later stages so abrupt and unexpected that there had been no opportunity to drive the cattle to higher ground, which in nine-tenths of the cases was miles away."*[103]

In an ironic twist, the Missouri River lost one. It changed course and straightened out a curve, saving the steamboats seventeen miles on their future trips.

> *"The subsidence of the flood left the bottom lands strewn with blocks of ice, in all dimensions, frequently four feet thick; the sloughs or low places filled with water and crossable only with boats; haystacks swept away, live stock drowned and floated off with the current, and over one-half the buildings wrecked or altogether destroyed.*
>
> *...The big bend in the Missouri River a few miles above Vermillion was cut off by the flood of 1881, and the Missouri shortened just about seventeen miles... The new channel will save the steamboats eighteen miles, less a half."*[104]

The *Dakota Herald* was a newspaper published at Yankton, South Dakota, about twenty-five miles upriver from Vermillion. On April 2, 1881, they ran an emotional account about the catastrophe that had hit their town.

> *"For ten days the Missouri River valley for hundreds of miles has been covered with a seething torrent of water and ice. Whole towns have been absolutely obliterated, many lives have been lost, property incalculable has been swept away, and hundreds of people but yesterday in comparative affluence are to-day little else than beggars."*[105]

After that moving summary, the article then gave the disturbing details.

> "The river, at this point long watched with fear and trembling, at four o'clock Saturday afternoon, with scarcely a preliminary sign, Burst its icy covering, and in a few moments the whole channel was one mass of heaving, groaning, grinding cakes of ice, tossed and tumbled into every conceivable shape by the resistless current.
>
> "As the ice broke up the river rose with almost incredible rapidity, and in a few moments was nearly bank full. The steamer Western, lying just below the ways, was the first victim of the ice. An immense cake was hurled against her side near the stern, making a hole nearly twenty feet long, through which the water rushed in with terrible swiftness, and in spite of the efforts of a large corps of pumpmen, she soon filled and sank."

The remains of several ships sunk at that time are still in the Missouri river, and at times of low water, one is even visible from the Meridian Bridge.[106] This flood destroyed ships that were never replaced and marked the end of steamboat dominance in shipping. Afterward, even though it was still called shipping, their cargoes were carried by the railroad.

Yankton is not only on the river, but is also just upstream from where the James River meets the Missouri. With the convergence of the two flooded rivers, all the surrounding bottomland was flooded, regardless of which river did the flooding.

> "The water began to subside about five o'clock, and the people breathed easier, thinking that the worst was over. However, the

upward movement soon commenced again and continued all day Monday, the whole bed of the river being constantly filled with moving ice.

Monday afternoon word was received that the whole Jim River bottom below the city was overflowed from bluff to bluff, something never before known. This report was quickly succeeded by another to the effect that many families were completely cut off from escape and in need of assistance. Tuesday morning several boats were sent from the city, which succeeded in rescuing several families."

Residents fled from the bottoms to the bluffs above the river and could hardly take in what they saw.

"Many of our citizens on Tuesday took occasion to visit the bluffs, at Major Hanson's place, and the view there presented was truly grand, not to say terrible. As far as the eye could reach was an unbroken volume of water, moving steadily along, bearing on its bosom huge cakes of ice and dotted here and there by half-submerged farm houses, whose inmates had fled to the hills for safety.

Where the mighty current swept across the railroad track the rails were twisted and dragged long distances by the ice, while telegraph poles, fence posts and small trees were snapped in two like tallow candles.

Cattle and horses were floundering and struggling in the flood; every cake of ice was freighted with a passenger-list of small animals, while here and there a skiff, manned with rescuers from Yankton, paddled about from house to house after straggling persons who had been caught by the water. It was a spectacle long to be remembered, and one that a man might pray never to behold again."

That evening the ice again formed a dam.

"Tuesday evening at five o'clock, the ice which had been sweeping by all day suddenly formed a gorge a few miles below the city, which held firm all night, meanwhile extending itself far up the river toward Springfield...

Suddenly, Wednesday morning at 11:30 o'clock, a shudder ran through the vast body of the gorge where great hillocks of ice were piled in solid layers rods in height... [W]ith a sudden jerk the whole tremendous mass began to rear and crash and tumble... As the millions upon millions of tons of ice matter moved off down the river, the water began to creep up the banks.

Up, up it came, faster and faster, until it could fairly be seen to crawl up the ascent. Huge cakes of ice went hurtling against the sides of the steamers along the ways, crushing great holes in their hulls, snapping immense hawsers and precipitating the Black Hills, Helena and Butte into one common jumble. Still it rose, pouring over the railroad track, hurling the little ferryboat, Livingston, clear across it, and even carrying the gigantic Nellie Peck and Penina far upon the bank... [T]he torrent poured into the lower part of the city, actually seeming to have a fall of from six inches to a foot directly out of the river."

Apparently a number of people had not fled the town, in spite of the obvious danger. When the water came in, then they willingly fled.

"People ran hither and thither in wild excitement. Household goods were hastily thrown into wagons and removed to places of safety. Shouting, swearing men; weeping women and children; pawing, frightened horses... As the waters rose higher and higher, skiffs, yawls and other small craft began to shoot through the streets in lieu of wheeled vehicles. Furniture, clothing and babies were hauled out of the windows and ferried to high ground. Out houses and movable truck danced around on the surface. Hogs and chickens squealed and squawked, and swam and flew to places of safety.

All through the lower part of the city, everywhere in fact below the bench, roared an angry, surging torrent of yellow water, from one to six feet in depth... Looking south and east, it was a solid river ten miles wide... Down the channel of the river swept hay-stacks, water-tanks, live animals and the fragments of fences, houses, etc. which had been swept from, God knows where, up the river.

Far over on the Nebraska bottoms could be seen clusters of cattle on every knoll, and as the water rose inch by inch and the ice swept over and crushed them between its ponderous fragments, the struggles of the poor animals could be distinctly seen. Great trees, struck by the jagged chunks, whipped and shook as though jarred by a heavy wind, and finally would be cut clean off and tumbled into the seething hell of waters which roared about them.

Here and there appeared a roof of a house, and alas, in too many instances that roof held human beings clinging to it in a desperate effort to save themselves from a watery grave."

A week later the *Dakota Herald* updated events.

> "[A]fter the great rise of Wednesday, the 30th ult., which inundated lower Yankton and the Jim River bottoms and swept the town of Green Island out of existence in a few hours, the river fell rapidly back into its banks. Through Thursday, Friday and Saturday it remained with but little change, although constantly filled with floating ice in greater or lesser quantities.
>
> On Sunday morning, however, it commenced to rise rapidly, owing to the gathering of the ice a few miles below the city. The water continued to come steadily up all day, the gorge meanwhile extending itself up the river with amazing swiftness. Towards evening, people living in the lower part of the city, who had moved back after the falling of the first rise, again began to move out; and that their fears were well grounded was proven on Monday morning when the waters again covered all that portion of the city below the bench.
>
> All day Monday the gorge held firm, with the exception of intervals of a moment or two, when it would groan and heave and move a few rods down the stream, only to become stationary again. The water rose steadily all the time.
>
> The gorge continued all night Monday and Tuesday... At last, on Tuesday evening at four o'clock, the mighty wall of ice suddenly gathered itself for a last assault, and then with a resounding roar gave way... The water fairly leaped up, and in a few moments had reached its highest altitude since the beginning of the flood.
>
> ...By ten o'clock the water was out of the city limits, and by Wednesday morning the streets were again passable.

...Everything moveable had been swept away. But looking toward the river bank, where huge mountains of ice reared their heads twenty feet in the air, the people could well afford to be thankful. Had that shore gorge given completely away, and allowed the heaving channel, which watchers say was at times ten feet higher than the shore, to sweep through the city, it is doubtful if a building would have been left standing in the inundated region, or a steamer at the levee."[107]

Of course, since the snow pack was so widespread the flood was also far reaching. Farther downstream on the Missouri River, Omaha, Nebraska and Council Bluffs, Iowa were flooded in the Great Flood of 1881. Near Council Bluffs, the river changed course, leaving Lake Manawa in the old channel, which is now a state park. Around Fargo, North Dakota, the Red River flooded, as it often does, but with even greater force. Illinois and Wisconsin suffered floods, as did all points downriver on the Missouri, including Kansas City.

The other part of that great river system, the Mississippi, also caught the snow melt. That great river had been chosen as the natural boundary between the states of Illinois and Missouri. Kaskaskia, located on the Mississippi south of St. Louis, had been a prominent town in Illinois. It was the first capital of the state and had a population of several thousand by the early 1800's. In the flood of 1881, though, with its waters covering a wide area, the Mississippi changed course. Not only was Kaskaskia devastated by the flood, but when the river moved, the town wound up on the Missouri side. In the 2010 census, the town only retained fourteen residents and it is still an Illinois community on the Missouri side of the Mississippi.[108]

The incredible winter of 1880-81, with its extreme temperatures, monumental snow fall, continuous blizzards and devastating flooding was something the earlier residents of the plains, going back several generations, had never experienced.

> *"Strike-the-Ree, chief of the Yankton Indians, testified at the time that he had lived on the banks of the Missouri since 1801, and he had never witnessed nor had he learned of any similar flood, so it could not have been known to his father or to his father's father, for Indians have a custom of transmitting an account of such calamities through many generations. The ice in the Missouri River had frozen to the depth of three feet and over forty inches in many places, and it averaged in thickness, as was observed during the flood, nearly thirty inches.[109]"*

This chief knew of no such weather in his time, or that of his father or grandfather, which would go back to about 1750.

> *"Strike-the-Ree sent the following letter to "the paper at Yankton that gives all the news": It is now eighty winters that I have seen the snows fall and melt away along this Missouri River but I never saw a winter of such snows and floods as these.*
>
> *Spotted Tail, chief of the Brules, stated that there was nothing in the traditions of the Sioux Nation, or in the recollection of the oldest people of the tribe, going back practically to the beginning of the century, that could recall a winter as severe as that of 1880-81."*

Nobody could recall any winter as bad as the long, hard winter. And you know what?

Nobody remembers a winter as hard since that time, either.

~~~~~

Chapter 8

The Long, Hard, Black, Snow, Flood, Whatever Winter

So what was the long winter really like?

It was an incredible, agonizing, awful winter.

Winters on the Dakota frontier had a reputation for being rough. The *Challenge of Life on the Prairie* talks about –

the challenge of life on the prairie, naturally enough, including the hard winters.

> "*There is a commonly held misconception that, up until 1887, Dakota Territory had for many years experienced a series of relatively mild winters, thus giving those who settled in the region a false sense of security. But meteorological accounts of the winters during the 1870s and 1880s suggest otherwise. The country experienced especially harsh winters in:*
>
> *1873–1874 (Herds of cattle buried, snow covered buildings)*
>
> *1874–1875 (Congress appropriated $150,000 in relief aid for Dakota; 1/3 of the homesteaders in Polk County, Minnesota, abandoned their claims the following spring)*
>
> *1876–1877 (Two months of consecutive below zero days.)*"[110]

So it's not exactly like the hard winter caught them totally by surprise. Frontier settlers expected hard winters.

But not that hard!

Was the winter of 1880-81 really as bad as Laura pictured in her book?

Really!

St. Paul, Minnesota is one state east of South Dakota, about 250 miles from De Smet. During the winter of 1880-81, accurate records were relatively sparse. The United States Army Signal Corps had stations around the country where they took daily measurements of temperature, wind and precipitation. Snowfall depths were not recorded, other than as amount of precipitation when melted.

Charles J. Fisk of the United States Navy has written a number of academic papers doing statistical analysis on weather related elements. He authored *"A Multivariate Analysis of Summary-of-the-day Snowfall Statistics vs. Same-day Water Precipitation and Temperature Recordings."* Based on that, he calculated from recorded precipitation totals the estimated seasonal snowfall for St. Paul for the winter of 1880-81.

Fisk wrote,

> *"The 1880-81 snow-season commenced early, in mid-October, with some six inches (estimated) falling in St. Paul over the 16th-18th, severe blizzard-like conditions prevailing over the western portions of the state."*

A six inch snowfall is not that heavy. Therefore when the October Blizzard hit, St. Paul may have missed the worst part of the storm. The University of Minnesota has a list of their most famous winter storms and the October blizzard made the list. *"October 16, 1880, earliest blizzard in Minnesota, struck [southwest] and [west central] counties. Huge drifts exceeding 20 ft in the Canby area last until the next spring."*[111]

In his analysis, Charles Fisk continued,

> *"November was one of the coldest in Minnesota history, 20.6" total snowfall estimated for St. Paul from the models."*

The following records from that November still stand for lowest daily temperatures in St. Paul/Minneapolis.

Nov 17, 1880 – record low -5

Nov 21, 1880 – record low -11

Nov 22, 1880 – record low -6

Nov 25, 1880 – record low -18.

So that November was one of the coldest in Minnesota history and they got nearly two feet of snow, piled on top of the still frozen October snow.

In Vermillion, South Dakota, by the end of November the Missouri River was frozen thick enough for teams to cross. The editor of their newspaper the *Standard* wrote on Dec. 4:

> *"We have already had six weeks of good solid winter, something that never occurred before in the memory of the oldest inhabitant."*

Although they already had six weeks of winter by the end of November, winter was just getting started. *"December likewise very snowy with 33.0 inches approximated,"* Fisk calculated.

The October snow never had a chance to melt. The snows of November brought bitter cold, so they never melted, either. By the time December came along, the temperatures are seasonally cold, anyway. Meaning that by the end of December, St. Paul and the upper Midwest had received about four and a half feet of snow, and most of it was still there and not going anywhere.

What they needed was a break in the weather. What they got was record-breaking weather.

> *"The winter's outstanding month, however, was January,"* Fisk continued, *"with an estimated 57.1", derived from 4.34" of water-equivalent precipitation. The 57.1" estimated snowfall figure ... is more than 10" greater than the current-day Minneapolis-St. Paul individual monthly record of 46.9" for November 1991."*

So, on top of about four feet of snow on the ground, they then got the largest monthly snowfall ever recorded – a full ten inches more than anything seen in any month since 1881. Not only was it a record-breaking snow month, but it was almost a foot more than any other month in the last one-and-a-quarter centuries. January has thirty-one days, and snow fell on sixteen of those days.

And guess what? It was cold.

> *"January 1881 was a cold month, the mildest daily mean for a snow-day only 25.5 F,"* Fisk wrote.

Incredibly, January nearly doubled the snow that was already on the ground. The area had received about sixty inches already, and another fifty-seven inches piled on top of that, giving a total of one-hundred-seventeen inches, or about ten feet of snow. Remember this was not in one small locality, as a lake effect snow might be. This snow was all over the northern Midwest and beyond.

What do you do with ten feet of snow on the ground?

Not a whole heck of a lot.

As snow piles on itself, it melts a little now and then from the radiant heat of the sun, and the sheer weight of the snow compresses it somewhat, which lessens the overall depth. However, if you take ten feet of snow and compact it down by half, what are you looking at?

Snow.

The snow winter was not through snowing, though.

> "*In February, another 27.7" of snow "came", March "receiving" 7.0" and April 0.2", respectively,*" Fisk said.

In contrast to this comparatively light snow in March in St. Paul, some areas received their worst storms of the winter in March. Since the October blizzard was worse to the west and since they did not get their worst storms in March, St. Paul may have been on the light end of the snowfall!

The *Milwaukee Journal,* in an October 15, 1922 article recalling the snow winter, said,

"The big snow came in March. For three days and two nights there was a constant heavy downfall of snow which the winds heaped into drifts 40 feet high and covered trees growing in low places up to their tips."[112]

Nevertheless, St. Paul definitely had a good crop of snow that year.

"Signal Corps records for St. Paul for the snow winter shows that the area received almost fifteen inches of precipitation from the middle of October through the middle of April."

Again, snowfall depths were not recorded; only precipitation amounts of melted snowfall. A rule of thumb is that one inch of water equals ten inches of snow. That means that St. Paul got about one-hundred-fifty inches of snow that winter. Using a more complicated formula developed by Fisk gives a snowfall total of about one-hundred-forty-one inches. The obvious:

"Snowfall for this season was extraordinarily heavy... exceeding the modern-era 1983-84 official seasonal snowfall record for Minneapolis-St. Paul (98.6") by more than 50 percent."

Take the snowiest winter ever seen in the area since that time, with eight feet of snow, then take half of that snowfall – four feet – and shovel it on top of the pile and you have the winter of 1880-81. Mile after mile, state after state, homestead after homestead covered with twelve feet of snow.

One state south of South Dakota, in Brown County, Nebraska, the hard winter was remembered like this.

> *"The winter of 1880-'81 has gone into history as one of the most severe that was ever known. The prairies were covered with snow so deep that the cattle could not graze on the buffalo grass on which the ranchers relied for their winter feed. The snow came early in the fall and laid on the ground all winter. It was so deep that the cattle could not travel, and at times a crust of ice covered the surface of it making travel impossible as the cattle sank into the snow and thousands of head starved to death, sometimes in sight of the hay which ranchers had put up to be fed when the cattle could not graze.*
>
> *Of the 3,000 head on the Cook ranch only 800 were left in the spring. Other ranchers had similar losses and were obliged to close out, thus leaving the fertile prairies open to settlement by the farmers who came a few years later."*[113]

Far to the west in Idaho and Washington, after the hard winter cattle bones littered the landscape.

> *"Ranchers followed miners into the interior Columbia Basin, particularly following the discovery of gold in the Clearwater River Basin of Idaho in 1860. Most of the ranchers settled around Walla Walla, where there were gently rolling hills covered with grass and the climate seemed favorable to raising livestock. Farther east the land was more hilly; farther north it was more barren and rocky. Well-used trails passed through the area, and the Columbia was nearby for access to transportation and water.*
>
> *Soon the industry flourished, but the climate proved to be unfavorable, particularly the winters. Temperatures routinely dropped to zero and below, and winds would rake the region for days on end. The winter of 1861-62 was harsh. Ninety percent of the cattle in the Walla Walla area — about 9,000 — died.*

The winter of 1880-81 was similarly hard, and the bones of dead livestock were visible on the prairies for years afterward. That winter devastated the industry, and only a few herds remained."[114]

In Iowa, southeast of the little town on the prairie, they called the hard winter the starvation winter.

"The winter of 1880-81 is known in the annals of Remsen (Iowa) as the "starvation winter," it might also be termed the "freeze-out winter," because if hunger did beset the little garrison, none the less did the lack of fuel cause much trouble. Those who remember the serious inconveniences of the long snow blockades, even in a much larger town, can imagine the sufferings of those who were ten miles from a grocery store, the same distance from a meat market, and who did not live on a farm, consequently did not have a well filled cellar to fall back on."[115]

The *Columbus Journal* of Columbus, Nebraska, in a January 05, 1881 article, talked about the long reach of the long winter. Little did they know that by January, they were only halfway through!

"The cold wave visited other portions of the union besides Nebraska. Reports from New York, Illinois, Georgia, Missouri, Dakota, District of Columbia. South Carolina, Virginia, Louisiana, Mississippi, Indiana, Ohio, Alabama and North Carolina, give an unusual slate of the weather in the amount of snow and the extreme cold for certain localities. It is said that the snow in North Carolina is the heaviest and most severe known for twenty years, and in Alabama the heaviest ever known. The thermometer marked lower in Louisiana than ever

known and the greatest snowfall. Three snow storms occurred lest (sic) week in Virginia and snow now blocks the roads and stops travel." [116]

Even on the east coast of the US, where the Atlantic Ocean tends to lessen temperature swings, the weather was severe, as the weather service says.

"December 30 1880-January 1, 1881: The "New Years Deep Freeze" began with parts of western and central Maryland receiving nearly two feet of snow. The fresh snow aided in plummeting temperatures. The coldest temperatures occurred between December 30, 1880, and January 1, 1881. Baltimore dropped to -6F, Emmitsburg -19F, and Woodstock (Howard County) -17F.

Washington, DC recorded low temperatures of -7F on the 30th, -13F on the 31st, and -14F on New Year's Day. Only the "Great Arctic Outbreak" in February 1899 would be colder than this episode." [117]

John Burroughs was one of America's most noted nature essayists, in the vein of Ralph Waldo Emerson. He lived about a hundred miles north of New York City. Observing nature, he couldn't help but note the effect of the unnatural winter of 1880-81.

"Such a winter as was that of 1880-81 — deep snows and zero weather for nearly three months — proves especially trying to the wild creatures that attempt to face it. The supply of fat (or fuel) with which their bodies become stored in the fall is rapidly exhausted by the severe and uninterrupted cold, and the sources from which fresh supplies are usually obtained are all

but wiped out. Even the fox was very hard pressed and reduced to the un- usual straits of eating frozen apples; the pressure of hunger must be great, indeed, to compel Reynard to take up with such a diet."[118]

However, being a lover of nature, he also could not help noting a sweet spot in that year, that being sweeter smelling flowers.

"Some hepaticas are sweet-scented and some are not, and the perfume is stronger some seasons than others. After the unusually severe winter of 1880-81, the variety of hepatica called the sharp-lobed was markedly sweet in nearly every one of the hundreds of specimens I examined."[119]

In her book *The First Four Years,* Laura often used the phrase, "The rich have their ice in the summer, but the poor get theirs in the winter." That winter, everybody got ice. Record amounts of ice were harvested from the rivers and lakes for use the next summer.

Appleton's Annual Cyclopaedia says,

"In 1870 there were about 250,000 tons of ice harvested on the Kennebec River, at a cost of about a dollar a ton. The amount has grown annually, until it reached its maximum in 1880, when 1,000,000 tons were stored on the Kennebec [in Maine] and its vicinity. Last winter, owing to the intense cold weather which prevailed all over the country, and which made a good ice- crop on the Hudson, and in the ponds in Massachusetts and New York, but about 600,000 tons were stored on the river, at a cost for harvesting of from fifteen to twenty-five cents a ton."[120]

In Nova Scotia, Canada, that winter was even harder than Canadian winters are supposed to be.

> "Winter of 1880-81, one of the hardest ever seen in Nova Scotia with snow reaching the tops of the telegraph poles in places. Residents either stayed home or traveled by snowshoes or dog sled. In some places horse and sled or ox and sled were unable to make their way."[121]

Way down south in Arkansas, the weather is usually so warm that it slows down the speaking and all the vowels have two syllables. However, L. J. Kalklosch wrote a book in 1881 about the interesting little town of Eureka Springs, and he had to mention the hard winter just past.

> "The winters are very mild, and last but a few months. Snow does not often fall to the depth of even a few inches, and then it is transient. December and January are generally the winter months, and frequently, they pass without much blustering. It is true there are a few exceptions.
>
> The winter of 1880-81 was a remarkably cold one, even in the "Sunny South." Old settlers say they "never saw the like." The writer saw several winters in Ohio even much milder than this was in Arkansas. But it was an exception, and another such visitation may not come for century hence.
>
> ...The winter was an unusual one. Never was the weather so severe and the winter so long as this, in the recollections of the oldest settlers in this latitude.
>
> Owing to the extreme cold weather but little building or improving was done during the winter. And as the weather

was more severe than people had anticipated many were not prepared to protect themselves from the cold, and in consequence, there was much suffering among the poorer class."[122]

How about a trip to the Arctic during that winter?

The ship *Jeannette* carried a party that sailed for the Arctic in 1879 to try to reach the North Pole. The ship was trapped in the ice and a rescue ship was sent a couple of years later.

Appleton's Cyclopaedia says of the rescue ship,

> "The steamer sailed June 16th, and put in during a storm at Reikiavik, Iceland, July 9th. They learned that the winter there had been the severest one recorded since 1610. The Arctic ice still approached to within thirty miles of the north coast. Reports of the extreme rigor of the winter of 1880-'81 from other parts of the Arctic regions increased the general anxiety as to the fate of the Jeannette's party.
>
> In parts of the coast of Hudson Bay the cold was reported to have been of unprecedented intensity, and was said to have been unusually severe also at different points in Siberia."[123]

The Jeannette crew began with 33 men. Only 13 survived. That was not a good time to be in the Arctic.

How about on the other side of the pond?

The *Waukesha Freeman*, in their article "Winter of the Big Snow," had an interesting tidbit.

> *"One day the Milwaukee operator wired along the line the Cable news that it had just snowed steadily in Scotland for seventy hours."*[124]

A book published in Scotland shortly after the winter of 1880-81 contained these notes.

> *"Heavy fall of snow in NE Scotland in the 2nd week of October. Unusually, an early heavy snowfall between 19th and 20th October, 1880. This snowfall mainly affected southern England for up to 12 hours in places. 30 cm of snow fell at Sevenoaks, Kent and 20 cm at Crowborough, E. Sussex. 15 cm fell in other areas of Kent, as well as London and Surrey, damaging oak and elm trees as foliage was still upon many trees.*
>
> *Also heavy snow and severe frost in December - the latter being noted at the time as the most intense for 50 years. The harsh conditions continued into early New Year 1881.*
>
> *The easterly blizzard between the 18th and 20th in 1881 was most intense in central southern counties of England (Dorset, Wiltshire, and the Isle of Wight) giving about 1 meter* (thirty-nine inches) *of level snow in the Isle of Wight with heavy drifting. (One of the greatest on modern record). Affected the whole of England, except far north.*
>
> *About 100 people lost their lives and most businesses were halted for a day. Plymouth deprived of water for a week, and it took about a week before road and rail travel returned to normal. In London, the snow depth was about 25cm, with 1m drifts. Possible 5m drift in Oxford Circus. 2 m drifts in Portsmouth. 45cm depth in Brighton, 30cm in Exeter and on Dartmoor, as much as 100 cm."*[125]

During that winter the south end of Loch Lomond froze over, an event worth noting in Scottish history, and was filled with thousands of skaters."[126]

So there was a silver lining in the bad weather. The skating was great.

The *Times* of London ran an article on Jan 20, 1881, about the Great Blizzard that had just blanketed Great Britain.

> *"There is now only too much reason to conjecture that the information which reached the metropolis before telegraph lines were blown down or trains snowed up did not fully represent the extent of the mischief done by the storm. The wind moderated but slightly on Tuesday night in London, and additional falls of snow made the accumulation so great that the remarkable spectacle was presented yesterday morning where the wind had full play of houses literally blocked up with 5ft. and 6ft. of snow, the main thoroughfares and portions of the numerous lines of railway in and near the metropolis in a similar plight, and the traffic generally at a standstill.*
>
> *Though, however, the snow still descended, accompanied by half a gale of wind from the eastward, the fall bore no comparison with that beaten about in every direction by the hurricane of the previous day, and in all parts the shovel was brought into requisition. In the City and West-end several hundreds of men were early engaged in the work of clearing the blocked up roadways, and the streets soon promoted a more lively aspect."*

We will simply note that the snowfall was so severe that in all parts of London the shovel was brought into requisition. The

Times also reported that seventy to eighty barges went down in the River Thames on that Tuesday, some with loss of life.

The storm included heavy snow and wind, just like a Midwest blizzard, as the *Times* notes from surrounding areas indicates.

> *"BIRMINGHAM, 19TH. – The entire gable end of a house was blown out, and the roof of a church destroyed by the fall of a large chimney."*

> *"BOURNEMOUTH, JAN 19. A second fall of snow today has rendered vehicular and passenger traffic very difficult, and in some parts of the district wholly impossible. The snow in many of the drifts is now quite six feet deep."*

England has a northerly latitude but not a severe climate as would be seen with such a latitude in North America. The Gulf Stream flows from the Gulf of Mexico along the east coast of America, then over to the British Isles and moderates their winters. Such a snow as fell in 1881 was very unusual, and, as in the Midwest, was deep enough to prevent powerful locomotives from breaking through.

> *"BRISTOL, JAN. 19. – The gale abated during the night, but the snowfall continued so heavily that this morning all traffic was suspended, the snow lying deep even in the central streets, while the roads outside the city were impassable...Nearly all the lines of railway coming into Bristol are more or less blocked, but the section of the Great West between Bath and this city has been kept open. A portion of the North mail arrived here at 1 o'clock in the day, but it took six or seven locomotives to bring in on from Cheltenham."*

> "EXETER, JAN. 19 – The fall of snow has continued almost without intermission since yesterday morning, and today the gale has been very severe. The average depth of the snow is about 2ft., but in many drifts 4ft. and 5ft. deep. Country roads are almost impassable… One train came through from Okehampton to Exeter, but was eight hours doing the journey of less than 20 miles."

Let's see – twenty miles in eight hours is a speed of two and a half miles per hour for that train, equal to a slow walk. But the train did get through!

Needless to say, that Tuesday was not a great day for a funeral.

> "DUBLIN, JAN. 19. – A mourning coach which was returning from a funeral yesterday from Swords to Dublin was overwhelmed by a snowdrift, the carriage, horses, and coachman being completely enveloped, and but for the timely assistance of some men from a neighboring farm, who released the horses and man, the consequences might have been fatal to all. The coach had to be left covered with snow until today, when a staff of 12 men with shovels had to be sent to the scene of the snowdrift to extricate it. The men had to dig for 50 yards before they found the coach."

As in the US, that incredible winter claimed lives.

> "NEWBURY, JAN. 19 – Two casualties have been reported to the district coroner. One occurred at Cold Ash, where a man named George Hawkins, in charge of a horse and cart, and was snowed up, and buried alive just as he was approaching his home. At Inkpen a man was found today in the snow quite dead."

Quite dead.

In another accident, one train ran into a second, because neither could see through the snow.

> "WINDSOR, JAN. 19 – Mr. Gardiner, assistant-superintendent, and a breakdown gang, left Staines with four couple locomotives, which proceeded safely along the down line to within a short distance of Datchet, when the foremost engine ran into a locomotive which had brought Mr. Cheeseman, the stationmaster, and a small staff from Windsor to clear the block. In the darkness and blinding snow neither party was aware of the proximity of the other, and the approach of the relieving engine was unperceived by the officials with the Windsor locomotive until it was too late to avert the catastrophe."

The *Times* summed up the storm in this way.

> "Rarely have we to register such intense frost and severe weather as that experienced during these past seven days. ... During the (Monday) night the wind's force rapidly increased, and the barometer, which hitherto had not varied much, began to fall quickly. This it continued to do on the following day (Tuesday), when we were visited by one of the most severe snow storms ever remembered to have occurred.
>
> Snow commenced here between 9 and 10 a.m. and was accompanied by a terrific gale of wind, which lasted without intermission all day. The anemometer at noon registered 60 miles in the hour, but some of the gusts must have far exceeded that rate. As late as 7 p.m. it was blowing an average hourly rate of 50 miles... It is impossible to get any idea of the average depth of the downfall, as owing to the extreme violence of the

> wind, the exposed places are comparatively clear of snow, whereas the drifts against obstructions are from 4ft. to 5ft. in depth.
>
> The provinces are even worse off than London is. We hear from all sides of interrupted traffic, of telegraph wires broken, of towns and villages snowed up, and with no near hope before them of renewed communication with the world outside. This has been the result of one day's storm, but it has been such a day as we have never before had experience of, and we may trust, by the rule of averages, that for the present generation it will be the last as well as the first of its kind. Black Tuesday will not soon be forgotten."

One long-term effect of the hard winter in Britain was the killing of trees, as the *Gardener's Monthly* points out.

> "The London World says, alluding we suppose to effects of the severe winter of 1880-81, which would now only the past summer show its full effects: "The destruction of trees on Lord Haddington's estate, in Haddingtonshire, was so wholesale that the beauty of his place is entirely destroyed, and it will be half a century before the loss can be replaced. Lord Haddington feels this so acutely that he has shut up his place and gone abroad for the winter, preferring this to watching the clearing away of the ruins, which will occupy many months.""[127]

Poor guy.

Europe also suffered the killing of trees, as the *Gardener's Monthly* notes.

> "[W]e consider the reports which come to us of the great losses among fruit trees in Europe by the winter of 1880-81.

> *It is a nice thing to have peaches to sell when your neighbor has not any. The winter of 1880-81, which destroyed so many fruit buds, made a fortune for the owner of trees which escaped and thus furnished a new illustration of the old story about the bad wind."*

In view of all that, was the winter of 1880-81 as bad as Laura pictured?

Actually, it was worse.

The blizzards may not have been quite as numerous as Laura said, but the extent of the winter went far beyond the little town on the prairie, as we have seen. However, there is one other factor that Laura did not include in *The Long Winter* that made it even worse than she said.

When the Ingalls spent that terrible winter in Pa's store building in De Smet, they had some freeloading moochers living with them.

Laura did not put this in her book. She did not like to say negative things about people, even if such things were true. But those people were there with the Ingalls during the hard winter, and they made it even harder.

William Masters had known the Ingalls family in Burr Oak, Iowa and Walnut Grove, Minnesota. Relations had been very friendly between them. He had hired Pa to do some work for him and Pa had built the Ingalls a house on a lot in Masters' pasture.

William's brother Sam Masters was the schoolteacher in

Walnut Grove. Laura remembered him as being "*tall and thin, with bad teeth and a bad breath and small brown eyes and a bald head.*"[128]

Again we point out that *Pioneer Girl* was written without adjustments of courtesy or charity. With that in mind, we get the definite impression that Laura did not think too highly of Sam Masters. She recalled that with his bad teeth and bad breath, he came too close when he talked to them, which is exactly what a person with bad breath and bad teeth ought not do. And he would "*absent-mindedly pick up and fondle any of the girls' hands that happened to be handy. He captured mine one day when I had a pin in my fingers and I turned the pin quickly, so it jabbed deep when he squeezed. After that he let my hands alone.*"[129]

Sam Masters had several children, including daughter Genevieve. Laura said that Genevieve "sneered" at her and the other schoolgirls because they were from the west. You may recall in the *Little House on the Prairie* television series, in the second episode, a certain young lady sneered at Laura and Mary and called them "country girls."

See if you can notice a resemblance between Genevieve and that young lady.

> "*She thought herself much above us because she came from New York. She was much nicer dressed then we were and lisped a little when she talked; if she could not have her way in anything she cried or rather sniveled. Everyone gave up to her and tried to please her because they liked to appear friends with the new girl.*"[130]

Genevieve was a sniveler.

Later Sam Masters moved his family, including sniveling Genevieve, to De Smet and claimed a homestead west of town. Genevieve was then one of Laura's classmates.

> *"Ida, Mary and I did try to be friendly to Genevieve but she still thought that being from New York made her far above common people, but after some slighting remarks and elevations of the nose we left her alone. Then she became "teacher's pet," spending all the playtime with her."* [131]

If the name Genevieve Masters does not seem familiar, but her personality does, this is why –

In the Little House® books, Genevieve Masters was one of the girls that Nellie Oleson was based on. There were at least two, another being named Nellie Owens. They each had their petulant points, and when the books were written Genevieve and Nellie were combined into one irritating antagonist.

Genevieve had an older brother, George. In the fall of 1880, George headed west past De Smet to find work. He asked the Ingalls to let his wife Maggie stay with them, to be closer to him.

While George went west, Maggie had his baby at the Ingalls. Then George came back to De Smet, and as winter set in – as the long, hard, snow winter set in – George, Maggie and the new baby lived with the Ingalls.

They did not ask to spend the winter with the Ingalls. The Ingalls did not ask them to spend the winter with them. But the three of them just kept living there, and the Ingalls were far too polite to suggest otherwise, of course.

But Laura did indicate that George was a lot like his father Sam, the close talker with bad breath and bad teeth. See if you can see the resemblance.

> *"We could not keep the whole house warm so we shut off the front room and kept the fire going in the kitchen stove, using it both for cooking and warmth. Mary had her rocking chair on one side, close up to the oven door and Maggie with her baby had a rocking chair in the other warm place on the other side of the stove, with the heat from the open oven door on her feet and knees and the baby in her lap.*
>
> *George would crowd next to Maggie getting part of the warmth from the oven, while the rest of us did the best we could. Grace sat most of the time in Mary's lap while Ma and Carrie and I hovered in front or crowded in at the back to stand between the stove and the wall, always giving Pa room when he came in from the chores, for Pa did all the chores while George sat by the fire.*
>
> *Pa would get up in the bitter cold and start the fire singing "Oh I am as happy as a big sunflower that nods and bends in the breezes," while George lay snug and warm in bed until breakfast was nearly ready. George was always first at the table at any meal and though the rest of us ate sparingly and fairly because food was scarce, he would gobble, not denying himself even for Maggie as we did because of her nursing the baby.*
>
> *As our potatoes became scarce, he would help himself first to them and hurry to eat them so quickly that he always burned himself on them. Then clapping his hands to his mouth he*

> would exclaim "Potatoes do hold the heat!" This happened so often the rest of us made a byword of it."[132]

The long winter was made a lot worse for the Ingalls because they were, in effect, boarding Nellie Oleson's freeloading brother!

On the other hand, how did the Ingalls go through that winter?

Notice.

> ""I suppose this is blocking the trains?" Ma said.
>
> "Well, we've lived without a railroad," Pa answered cheerfully, but he gave Ma the look that warned her to say no more about it while the girls were listening. "We're snug and warm, as we've been before without even the people and the stores," he went on."[133]

When Ma and Pa first realized that the trains were blocked and food would be scarce, their thoughts were not for themselves, but for their children.

On those cold mornings, when the water in the pail froze – inside the house! – Pa was first up to get the fire going. Laura mentioned in both *Pioneer Girl* and *The Long Winter* that he sang this song. "*Oh I am as happy as a big sunflower that nods and bends in the breezes.*"

We can easily figure out that Pa did not really relish getting up on those dark, frigid mornings to start his daily battle with the blizzards. Believe it or not, he was not really so happy that he just had to burst out in a song about sunflowers!

But he did it!

As soon as he got the fire going, he went out in the bitter cold to tend to the animals. On clear days, he drove a horse and sled to the homestead to haul more hay. The snow was so deep that the horse and sled ran on top of the frozen snow, until they fell through and had to be dug out.

When Pa got back inside the warm house, which was warm only if compared to the outside, he took the farthest spot from the stove and ate as little food as he could.

> "Pa was already in his place at the table, Mary was lifting Grace onto the pile of books in her chair, and Ma was setting a dish of steaming baked potatoes before Pa. "I do wish we had some butter for them," she said."
>
> "Salt brings out the flavor," Pa was saying..." [134]

Are potatoes really better without butter?

The entire Ingalls family shared Pa's attitude of not being selfish, such as when they insisted he take an extra potato, since he had to work hard outside.

> ""They're not big potatoes, Charles," [Ma] argued, "and you must keep up your strength. Anyway, eat it to save it. We don't want it, do we, girls?
>
> "No, Ma," they all said. "No, thank you, Pa, truly I don't want it."[135]

In the Ingalls family, each person was willing to put the others first.

When they came to the very last of the potatoes, they did not fuss over who would get it, but who would give it.

> ""I'm not hungry, honest, Pa," Laura said."I wish you'd finish mine."
>
> "Eat it, Laura," Pa told her, kindly but firmly.""[136]

Unlike George, Pa did not hog the potatoes, and neither did the rest of Pa's family. When they did not have enough, no one tried to get more for him or herself.

Laura volunteered to help Pa twist the hay into sticks to burn. The job was cold and uncomfortable, but why should Pa have to do it all? Finally, even blind Mary was led into the lean-to to twist hay, too. Each was willing to do her part.

While George sat in front of the warm fire digesting his potatoes.

Though they had little during that hard winter, the Ingalls were still thankful for what they did have. When the cow was nearly dry and the milk was running out, Ma said:

> ""Let's be thankful for the little milk we have," she said, "because there'll be less before there's more.""[137]

Thirty-five years after the hard winter, Laura was still thankful.

> "I read a Thanksgiving story, the other day, in which a woman sent her little boy out to walk around the block and look for something for which to be thankful.

One would think that the fact of his being able to walk around the block and that he had a mother to send him would have been sufficient cause for thankfulness. We are nearly all afflicted with mental farsightedness and so easily overlook the thing which is so obvious and near. There are our hands and feet, - who ever thanks of giving thanks for them, until indeed they, or the use of them, are lost. We usually accept them as a matter of course, without a thought, but a year of being crippled has taught me the value of my feet and two perfectly good feet are now among my dearest possessions. Why! There is greater occasion for thankfulness just in the unimpaired possession of one of the five senses that there would be if some one left us a fortune. Indeed how could the value of one be reckoned? When we have all five in good working condition we surely need not make a search for anything else in order to feel that we should give thanks to Whom thanks are due.

I once remarked upon how happy and cheerful a new acquaintance seemed always to be and the young man to whom I spoke replied, "Oh he's just glad that he is alive." Upon inquiry, I learned that several years before this man had been seriously ill, that there had been no hope of his living, but to everyone's surprise he had made a complete recovery and since then he had always been remarkably happy and cheerful."[138]

During the long winter, the Ingalls would not let themselves get discouraged. Being discouraged is focusing on the self, putting yourself first, feeling self-pity. Nobody ever helped anybody else by being discouraged. Once in the long winter Laura was discouraged over not getting to go to school because of the blizzards.

> "Now Laura," Ma said kindly. "You must not be so easily discouraged. A few blizzards more or less can make no great difference."[139]

You can't do your best if you are discouraged, Laura wrote in 1917.

> "Doing the best we can is all that could be expected of us in any case, but did you ever notice how hard it is to do our best if we allow ourselves to become discouraged? If we are disheartened, we usually lag in our efforts more or less. It is so easy to slump a little when we can give the blame to circumstances."[140]

In 1918, in the middle of the Great War, Laura wrote this.

> "If when anyone is in difficulty we would all help instead of taking advantage of their situation; if when trouble comes to those we know, we would do our utmost to make it lighter instead of gossiping unkindly about it; and if we would not be satisfied until we had passed a share of our happiness on to other people, what a world we could make!"[141]

The long winter was indeed terrible. Yet Laura's book about that terrible winter is a happy book. The Ingalls were as merry as merry could be, while cooped up in one room, burning hay for fuel, eating potatoes and brown bread with no butter, for months on end.

Laura later wrote about a readiness to laugh and be merry.

> "If the members of a home are ill-tempered and quarrelsome, how quickly you feel it when you enter the house. You may not know just what is wrong but you wish to make your visit

short. If they are kindly, generous, good-tempered people you will have a feeling of warmth and welcome that will make you wish to stay. Sometimes you feel that you must be very prim and dignified and at another place you feel a rollicking good humor and a readiness to laugh and be merry. Poverty or riches, old style housekeeping or modern conveniences do not affect your feelings. It is the characters and personalities of the persons who live there.

Each individual has a share in making this atmosphere of the home what it is, but the mother can mold it more to her wish. I read a piece of poetry several years ago supposed to be a man speaking of his wife and this was the refrain of the little story:

"I love my wife because she laughs,

Because she laughs and doesn't care."

I'm sure that would have been a delightful home to visit, for a good laugh overcomes more difficulties and dissipates more dark clouds than any other one thing. And this woman was the embodied spirit of cheerfulness and good temper.

Let's be cheerful! We have no more right to steal the brightness out of the day for our own family than we have to steal the purse of a stranger. Let us be as careful that our homes are furnished with pleasant and happy thoughts as we are that the rugs are the right color and texture and the furniture comfortable and beautiful!"[142]

Pa played the fiddle for them that winter with a warmth that came from the spirit and not from the hay in the stove. At night, the Ingalls marched upstairs into the unheated bedrooms to the beat of his fiddle jigs, the heat of the music carrying them step by step. Every day they said their prayers, when it seemed they weren't being answered, even though sometimes they got under the covers first. And during the lowest times, they sang the highest songs.

Jesus is a Rock

"Jesus is a rock in a weary land,
A weary land, a weary land,
Jesus is a rock in a weary land,
A shelter in the time of storm."

The Evergreen Shore

Then let the hurricane roar!
It will the sooner be o'er.
We'll weather the blast
And land at last
On Canaan's happy shore!"

When they all sang together of a shelter in the time of storm, singing loud enough to drown out a blizzard, don't you know that they really, really meant it.

Happiness does not come from getting for the self. Happiness comes from giving of the self. Laura well understood that.

> *"The person who keeps looking ahead for happiness is on the way to miss it, no matter how anxious and eager she is. The person who looks around for chances of making other people happy and carries them out, cannot escape being happy."*[143]

What a tremendous understanding of natural law. And this is that law, which Laura said is the highest code of honor yet voiced —

> *"Whatsoever ye would that men should do to you, do ye even so to them!"*[144]

That's what they tried to do that winter of 1880-81. The long winter, the hard winter, the snow winter, the Alpena winter, the starvation winter, the black winter –

That miserable stinking winter ultimately was a happy winter for the Ingalls! Because they all gave of themselves to the others.

And they even gave to the Masters.

The Masters took and did not give back. In response to that, the Ingalls gave and did not take. And they were so kind and gentle and giving that they never rebuked their selfish guests, all winter long. And when Laura wrote *The Long Winter*, she still gave to them by not including them in the story.

What was the long winter really like?

That winter deserved all its negative names. It reached to both sides of the Atlantic, and from the deep south to the Arctic.

What was the long winter really like?

That was a time of intense family closeness, of personal sacrifice, of showing love even at cost to oneself, of making merry when feeling sad, of encouraging when discouraged. For the Ingalls family, Pa and Ma and Mary, Laura, Carrie and

Grace, 1880-81 was a blessed, thankful year, with pure air, warmth, shelter, plain food and home folks.

> *"As the years pass, I am coming more and more to understand that it is the common, everyday blessings of our common everyday lives for which we should be particularly grateful. They are the things that fill our lives with comfort and our hearts with gladness—just the pure air to breathe and the strength to breathe it; just warmth and shelter and home folks; just plain food that gives us strength; the bright sunshine on a cold day and a cool breeze when the day is warm."*[145]

ENDNOTES

[1] Douglas Harper, *Online Etymology Dictionary*, "blizzard," http://www.etymonline.com/index.php?search=blizzard&searchmode=none.
[2] *Houghton Mifflin Word Origins*, "blizzard," http://www.answers.com/topic/blizzard.
[3] G.I. Gaston and A.R. Humphrey, *The History of Cuter Co. Nebraska*, "The Black Winter of 1880-81," (Lincoln, Nebraska: Western Publishing and Engraving Co., 1919), http://genealogytrails.com/neb/custer/weather.html.
[4] Bryan Yeaton, *The National Notebook* radio program, produced by the Mount Washington Observatory, March 8, 2004, http://www.weathernotebook.org/transcripts/2004/03/08.php.
[5] Edward Jensen, *Nordmaendene i Amerika*, translated by Martin Ulvestad, 1907, http://newsarch.rootsweb.com/th/read/NORWAY/2004-08/1093840631.
[6] *Milwaukee Journal*, "Fall Blizzard 42 Years Ago Began "Winter of the Big Snow," October 15, 1922, http://www.wisconsinhistory.org/wlhba/articleView.asp?pg=1&id=3670.
[7] *The Weekly South Dakotan*, Unit 6, "Lesson 2 Town Life and Hard Times," http://sd4history.com/Unit6/ hsandtblesson2.htm.
[8] Mrs. A. J. Wilder, *Missouri Ruralist*, "According to Experts," February 5, 1917.
[9] *New World Encyclopedia*, "Laura Ingalls Wilder," http://www.newworldencyclopedia.org/entry/Laura_Ingalls_Wilder
[10] Dan L. White, *Laura Ingalls' Friends Remember Her*, (Hartville, Mo.: Ashley Preston Publishing, 1992), 87.
[11] Wikipedia, "The Long Winter (novel)," http://en.wikipedia.org/wiki/The_Long_Winter_%28novel%29.
[12] Beatrice Wade Sipher, Personal journal entries compiled by Mary Wienbar, *Local History of Iroquois, S.D.* "History of Bancroft," http://iroquoissd.com/ local_history.htm.
[13] Randy A. Peppler, ""Old Indian Ways" of Knowing the Weather: Weather Predictions for the Winters of 1950-51 and 1951-52," University of Oklahoma, Norman, Oklahoma, ams.confex.com/ams/pdfpapers/143684.pdf .

[14] Brown County Territorial Pioneer Committee, *Early History of Brown County, South Dakota, A Literature of the People by Territorial Pioneers and Descendents*, (Aberdeen, SD: Western Printing Co., 1970), http://files.usgwarchives.net/sd/brown/ehbc/ehbc-1-30.txt.
[15] "The October Blizzard," http://www.pioneergirl.com/index.htm?tlw_fact.htm&Bot_Frame.
[16] George Kingsbury, *History of Dakota Territory*, Volume 2, (Chicago: S.J. Clarke Publishing Co., 1915), 1148.
[17] John Stanley, *Autobiography of John Stanley*, http://www.experiencegarysd.com/johnstanley.cfm.
[18] *Milwaukee Journal*, "Fall Blizzard 42 Years Ago Began 'Winter of the Big Snow.'"
[19] Cleo Erickson, *Vermillion Plain Talk*, Vermillion, SD, "After 1880, Vermillion and Big Mo Changed One went South, Other North," March 19, 2009, http://www.plaintalk.net/cms/news/story-46227.html.
[20] Daryl Ritchison, WDAY6 and WDAZ8 Storm Tracker, "The Long Winter," October 15, 2010, http://stormtrack.areavoices.com/2010/10/15/the-long-winter-2/.
[21] Constance Potter, *Prologue Magazine*, "Genealogy Notes: De Smet, Dakota Territory, Little Town in the National Archives, Part 2," "Homesteading, Eliza Jane Wilder," Winter 2003, Vol. 35, No. 4, http://www.archives.gov/publications/prologue/2003/winter/little-town-in-nara-2.html
[22] Laura Ingalls Wilder, *The Long Winter*, (New York: HarperCollins Publishers Inc., 1940), 2004 ed., 48.
[23] Michigan Shipwreck Research Associates, "The Alpena," http://www.michiganshipwrecks.org/alpena.htm.
[24] Ibid.
[25] Kathy Warnes, "The Lake Michigan Steamer Alpena Sinks in a Monster October Storm," Sep 26, 2010, http://www.suite101.com/content/the-lake-michigan-steamer-alpena-sinks-in-a-monster-october-storm-a290143.
[26] *Kingston Whig-Standard*, Ontario, "Marine Disasters – Results of a Fearful Gale," October 20, 1880, http://images.maritimehistoryofthegreatlakes.ca/58257/data?n=6.
[27] Michigan Shipwreck Research Associates, "The Alpena."
[28] Kathy Warnes, "The Lake Michigan Steamer Alpena Sinks in a Monster October Storm."
[29] Michigan Shipwreck Research Associates, "The Alpena."

[30] William Ratigan, *Great Lakes Shipwrecks & Survivals*, (Grand Rapids: Wm. B. Eerdman's Publishing Co., MI, 1977), 70.
[31] Kathy Warnes, "The Lake Michigan Steamer Alpena Sinks in a Monster October Storm."
[32] William Ratigan, *Great Lakes Shipwrecks & Survivals*, 71.
[33] Stu Beitler, "Holland, Mi (Lake Michigan–Unknown Location) Steamer Alpena Disaster, Oct 1880," http://www3.gendisasters.com/Michigan/15916/holland-mi-lake-michigan-unknown-location-steamer-alpena-disaster-oct-1880.
[34] *Kingston Whig-Standard*, October 21, 1880, http://images.maritimehistoryofthegreatlakes.ca/58257/data?n=6.
[35] Michigan Shipwreck Research Associates, "The Alpena."
[36] Benjamin Shelak, *Shipwrecks of Lake Michigan*, (Boulder, CO: Trails Books, 2003), 126.
[37] Mary Wienbar, *Local History of Iroquois, S.D.* "History of Manchester," http://iroquoissd.com/ local_history.htm.
[38] Ibid, "Early Iroquois Settlers."
[39] PBS, *Frontier House*, "Frontier Life," http://www.pbs.org/wnet/frontierhouse/frontierlife/essay4_3.html.
[40] Laura Ingalls Wilder, *Pioneer Girl*, unpublished memoir.
[41] Rebecca Brammer and Phil Greetham, "Cap Garland," http://liwfrontiergirl.com/garland.html
[42] *Waukesha Freeman*, "Winter of Big Snow in Waukesha Became Indelible in Lives of Local Residents Says Historian," May 1933.
[43] Mary Wienbar, *Local History of Iroquois, S.D.*, "The School Children's Blizzard of 1888."
[44] Dick Taylor, *Pawnee County History*, "BIG BRASH BLIZZARD OF 1888," http://www.pawneecountyhistory.com/yesteryear/blizzard.html
[45] Curt Nickish, *Weather Notebook*, "Schoolhouse Blizzard," http://www.weathernotebook.org/transcripts/2001/03/07.html
[46] Laura Ingalls Wilder, *Pioneer Girl*.
[47] Ibid.
[48] George Kingsbury, *History of Dakota Territory*, Vol. 2, 1157.
[49] Ibid., 1158.
[50] Ibid., 1149.
[51] John Stanley, *Autobiography of John Stanley*.
[52] George Kingsbury, *History of Dakota Territory*, Vol. 2, 1150.
[53] Ibid.

[54] L. B. Albright, Congregational United Church of Christ, http://ucc-cong-pierre.org/2006congucc-pierre/2006MomentsinourHistory.html.
[55] Doane Robinson, *History of South Dakota*, Vol. I, (Logansport, IN.: B.F. Bowen and Co., 1904), 306.
[56] Laura Ingalls Wilder, *Pioneer Girl*.
[57] Laura Ingalls Wilder, *Missouri Ruralist*, "Are We Too Busy?," October 5, 1917.
[58] Laura Ingalls Wilder, *Pioneer Girl*.
[59] Edward Jensen, *Nordmaendene i Amerika*.
[60] Doane Robinson, *History of South Dakota*, Vol. I, 306.
[61] Ibid.
[62] Pierre Chronicles, *Fort Pierre Times*, "Freighting In The 80's," February 17, 1937, 48-49, http://home.sodaklive.com/edocs/Hughes/hughes3.pdf.
[63] Laura Ingalls Wilder, *Pioneer Girl*.
[64] Ibid.
[65] Mary Wienbar, "Early Iroquois Settlers."
[66] Hiram Drache, *The Challenge of the Prairie: Life and Times of Red River Pioneers*, (Fargo: North Dakota Institute for Regional Studies, 1970), 150-153.
[67] Mary Wienbar, "History of Bancroft."
[68] *New York Times*, "Suffering Caused by Heavy Snow," March 15, 1881, http://query.nytimes.com/mem/archive-free/pdf?res=F10B1EF7395B1B7A93C4A81788D85F458884F9.
[69] John Stanley, *Autobiography of John Stanley*.
[70] Ibid.
[71] *Mini Bios of People of Scottish Descent*, "Peter Philip," http://www.electricscotland.com/history/world/bios/philp_peter.htm
[72] *Waukesha Freeman*, "Winter of Big Snow in Waukesha Became Indelible in Lives of Local Residents Says Historian."
[73] Doane Robinson, *History of South Dakota*, Vol. I, 306.
[74] John Stanley, *Autobiography of John Stanley*.
[75] Edward Jensen, *Nordmaendene i Amerika*.
[76] George Washington Kingsbury, *History of South Dakota*, Vol. II, (Chicago: S.J. Clarke Pub. Co., 1915), 1150.
[77] *Waukesha Freeman*, "Winter of Big Snow in Waukesha Became Indelible in Lives of Local Residents Says Historian."

[78] *Sheboygan Times*, "The Snow Storm of 1881," March 5, 1881, http://www.wisconsinhistory.org/wlhba/articleView.asp?pg=1&id=13038&key=snow&cy=
[79] George Washington Kingsbury, *History of South Dakota*, Vol. II, 1158.
[80] Ibid., 1157-1158.
[81] Laura Ingalls Wilder, *Pioneer Girl*.
[82] Laura Ingalls Wilder, *Missouri Ruralist*, "According to the Experts,"
[83] Alfred Lloyd Tennyson, *Locksley Hall*.
[84] *Waukesha Freeman*, "Winter of Big Snow in Waukesha Became Indelible in Lives of Local Residents Says Historian."
[85] Ibid.
[86] *Milwaukee Journal*, "Fall Blizzard 42 Years Ago Began "Winter of the Big Snow."
[87] *Waukesha Freeman*, "Winter of Big Snow in Waukesha Became Indelible in Lives of Local Residents Says Historian."
[88] Ibid.
[89] Ecclesiastes 3:1, *World English Bible*.
[90] *Early History of Brown County, South Dakota*.
[91] John Stanley, *Autobiography of John Stanley*.
[92] Ibid.
[93] Mary Wienbar, *Local History of Iroquois, S.D.*, "History of Manchester."
[94] Ibid., "The Winter of 1880-1881."
[95] Doane Robinson, *History of South Dakota*, Vol. I, 307.
[96] George Kingsbury, *History of Dakota Territory*, Volume II, 1151.
[97] Jill Callison, *Argus Leader*, Sioux Falls, S.D, "S.D. hasn't seen a flood like 1881," Mar 23, 2011, http://pqasb.pqarchiver.com/argusleader/access/2300541361.html?FMT=ABS&date=Mar+23%2C+2011.
[98] George Kingsbury, *History of Dakota Territory*, Volume II, 1152-1153.
[99] Ibid., 1153.
[100] Jill Callison, *Argus Leader*, Sioux Falls, S.D, "S.D. hasn't seen a flood like 1881."
[101] George Kingsbury, *History of Dakota Territory*, Volume II, 1153.
[102] Ibid. 1154.
[103] Ibid.
[104] Ibid., 1155.
[105] *Dakota Herald*, Yankton, S.D., April 2, 1881.
[106] Jennifer L. Nielson, *Yankton's History*, http://www.cityofyankton.org/yankton/history/index.php.

[107] *Dakota Herald*, Yankton, S.D., April 9, 1881.
[108] "Visitors Guide to Randolph County," http://www.greatriverroad.com/randhome.htm.
[109] George Kingsbury, *History of Dakota Territory*, Volume II, 1160.
[110] Hiram Drache, *The Challenge of the Prairie: Life and Times of Red River Pioneers*.
[111] Minnesota Climatology Working Group, "Famous Minnesota Winter Storms," http://climate.umn.edu /doc/historical/winter_storms.htm
[112] *Milwaukee Journal*, "Fall Blizzard 42 Years Ago Began "Winter of the Big Snow."
[113] "Winter of 1880-01, Brown County, Nebraska," http://www.nebraska genealogy.com/brown/winter2.htm.
[114] *Columbia River History*, "Livestock," http://www.nwcouncil.org/history/Livestock.asp.
[115] W.L. Clark, *Iowa Historical Record*, Vol. IX, No. 3, "Pioneer Days in Plymouth County," July 1893, http://iagenweb.org/plymouth/Cities/remsengermania.html.
[116] *Columbus Journal*; Columbus, Neb., January 5, 1881.
[117] Barbara McNaught Watson, *Maryland Winters, Snow, Wind, Ice and Snow*, "Maryland's Historic Winter Extremes," http://www.erh.noaa.gov/lwx/Historic_Events/md-winter.html.
[118] John Burroughs, *A Flower in a Woodland Roadway, Signs and Seasons*, (Boston and New York: Houghton Mifflin Company, 1886, 1895, 1914), 49.
[119] Ibid, 25.
[120] *Appletons' Annual Cyclopaedia and Register of Important Events of the Year 1881*, New Series Vol. 6, (New York: D. Appleton and Company, 1882), 527.
[121] Douglas Legere, *Acadian History Timeline*, "1875, Oct 10," http://doug legere.shawwebspace.ca /pages/view/acadian_history_timeline/.
[122] L.J. Kalklosch, *Healing Fountain,1879-81*, Chapter 1, "Discovery and General Aspect of the Country," http://books.eurekaspringshistory.com/1881_healing_fountain.htm.
[123] *Appletons' Annual Cyclopaedia and Register of Important Events of the Year 1881*, 324-325.
[124] *Waukesha Freeman*, "Winter of Big Snow in Waukesha Became Indelible in Lives of Local Residents Says Historian."
[125] *Meteorology @ West Moors, Historical Weather Events*, "1880 (Autumn/Early Winter)," "1881 (January)," http://booty.org.uk/booty.

weather/climate/1850_1899.htm.

[126] Loch Lomond, A historical perspective, drawn from the *Ordnance Gazetteer of Scotland: A Survey of Scottish Topography, Statistical, Biographical and Historical*, edited by Francis H. Groome and originally published in parts by Thomas C. Jack, Grange Publishing Works, Edinburgh between 1882 and 1885. Currently copyrighted by the editors of the *Gazetteer for Scotland*, 2002-2011.

[127] *The Gardener's Monthly and Horticulturist*, edited by Thomas Meehan, Vol. 24, (Philadelphia: Charles H. Marot, Publisher, 1882), 125.

[128] Laura Ingalls Wilder, Pioneer Girl.

[129] Ibid.

[130] Ibid.

[131] Ibid.

[132] Ibid.

[133] Laura Ingalls Wilder, *The Long Winter*, (New York: HarperCollins Publishers, 1940, revised 2007), 146.

[134] Ibid., 161.

[135] Ibid., 283.

[136] Ibid., 315.

[137] Ibid., 154.

[138] Mrs. A. J. Wilder. *Missouri Ruralist*, "Thanksgiving Time," November 20, 1916.

[139] Laura Ingalls Wilder, *The Long Winter*, 173.

[140] Mrs. A. J. Wilder. *Missouri Ruralist*, "Doing Our Best," June 5, 1917.

[141] Mrs. A. J. Wilder. *Missouri Ruralist*, "Santa Claus at the Front," January 20, 1918.

[142] Mrs. A. J. Wilder. *Missouri Ruralist*, "Thoughts are Things," November 5, 1917.

[143] Ibid.

[144] Mrs. A.J. Wilder. *Missouri Ruralist*, "Your Code of Honor," October 5, 1918.

[145] Mrs. A.J. Wilder. *Missouri Ruralist*, "As a Farm Woman Thinks," November 15, 1922.

Other books by Dan L. White

Information available at danlwhitebooks.com
Email at mail@danlwhitebooks.com.
Find us on Facebook at Dan L White Books.

Laura's Love Story
The lifetime love of Laura Ingalls and Almanzo Wilder

Real love is sometimes stronger than the romance of fiction. Laura and Almanzo's love is such a story. From an unwanted beau – Almanzo – to a beautiful romance; from the heart wrenching tragedy of losing their home and little boy to heart felt passion; from trials that most do not endure to a love that endured for a lifetime –

Laura's Love Story is the true account of two young people who lived through the most trying troubles to form the most lasting love.

Better than fiction, truer than life, this is the love story that put the jollity in Laura's stories and is the final happy ending to her Little House books.

Laura Ingalls' Friends Remember Her
Memories from Laura's Ozark Home

– contains memories from Laura and Almanzo's close friends, Ozarkers who knew them around their home town of Mansfield, Missouri. We chat with these folks, down home and close up, about their good friends Laura and Almanzo.

Laura also joins in our chats because we include long swatches of her magazine writings on whatever subject is at hand. It's almost as if she's there talking with us. Her thoughts on family and little farms and what-not are more interesting than almost anybody you've ever talked to.

Plus the book contains discussions of –

> how Laura's Ozark life made her happy books possible;
> what made Laura's books so happy;
> whether her daughter Rose wrote Laura's books;
> and Laura's last, lonely little house.

Laura Ingalls' Friends Remember Her includes –

> her friends' recollections;
> Laura's writings from her magazine articles;
> and fresh discussions of Laura's happy books and her life.

Laura's readers should find these insights into the Little House life interesting and uplifting.

Devotionals with Laura
Laura Ingalls' Favorite Bible Selections;
What they meant in her life, what they might mean in yours –

Laura Ingalls Wilder was a wonderful writer and an eager Bible reader. After her death a list of her most cherished Bible selections was found in her Bible. *Devotionals with Laura* discusses these Bible passages, including:

How they might have fit in with Laura's life;
What they might mean in our lives;
How they affected the Little House books.

When Laura said that she read a certain passage at a time of crisis or discouragement in her life, what events might have caused her to do that? When was she in a crisis? When was she discouraged? What did she say in her writings about such a time?

We include excerpts from Laura's articles where she talked about such events. When we have done these *Devotionals with Laura*, meditated on the passages she meditated on, considered her words for life's critical times, and taken in deeply the very words of Almighty God, then we can begin to understand how Laura's little Bible helped shape the Little House books.

The Jubilee Principle
God's Plan for Economic Freedom

WND Books, available at wndbooks.com.

–examines the economic "long wave", a boom-and-bust cycle that happens roughly twice a century in free economies, and parallels the wisdom of the fifty-year Jubilee cycle in the Bible. *The Jubilee Principle* shows how God designed Israel's society with the Sabbath, festivals, land sabbath and Jubilee year. How would it be to live a whole life under that system? *The Jubilee Principle* points the way to true security.

Laura Ingalls Wilder's Most Inspiring Writings
Notes and Setting by Dan L. White

These sparkling works of Laura Ingalls Wilder came **before** *Little House on the Prairie*.

Laura Ingalls Wilder wrote the famous book *Little House on the Prairie*, from which the television show came. She also wrote eight other books that tell of her life as a girl on the American frontier between about 1870 and 1889. Before that, she wrote articles about small farms, country living and just living life. *Laura Ingalls Wilder's Most Inspiring Writings* is a collection of forty-eight of the most interesting and uplifting of these writings.

Within Laura's words are gems of down to earth wisdom. Amazingly, most of her comments mean just as much today as when she wrote them. These writings give us her philosophy of life and are the seed stock of Laura's prairie books.

Big Bible Lessons from Laura Ingalls' Little Books

The Little House® books by Laura Ingalls Wilder are lovable, classic works of literature. They contain no violence and no vulgarities, yet they captivate young readers and whole families with their warmth and interest.

They tell the life of young Laura Ingalls, who grew up on the American frontier after the Civil War. Laura was part of a conservative Christian family, and they lived their lives based on certain unchanging values – drawn from the Bible.

Big Bible Lessons from Laura Ingalls' Little Books examines the Bible principles that are the foundation of Laura's writing, the Ingalls family, and the Little House® books. Not directly stated in words, they were firmly declared in the everyday lives of the Ingalls family. While you enjoy Laura's wonderful books, this book and these Bible lessons will help you and your family also grow spiritually from them.

The Real Laura Ingalls
Who was Real, What was Real on her Prairie TV Show

Fans of the **Little House on the Prairie** TV show know it was taken from Laura Ingalls Wilder's books. They know those books told the real story of Laura's life. But most have never read her books. Then they wonder ––

- What really happened?
- Who was real? Who wasn't?
- What stories on the show were like the stories in her books?

This book tells you just that.

The Real Laura Ingalls is for those fans of the show who have never read Laura's books and want to know how the show's stories connect with Laura's real life.

They do connect! From Almanzo to Nellie Oleson to sister Mary, the connection between the show's stories and Laura's stories is a fascinating story in itself. *The Real Laura Ingalls* tells this story in a fast moving, easy reading, crystal clear style, while upholding the values of the show and the books.

Reading along with Laura Ingalls in the Big Wisconsin Woods

Little House in the Big Woods fans can now enjoy that beloved story a little more.

Reading along with Laura Ingalls in the Big Wisconsin Woods delves a little deeper into Pa's stories about panthers and bears and honey bee trees, the dance at Grandpa's house, going into the town of Pepin, and the other goings-on in Laura's book.

Read along and discover how Laura wrote her book and how the times were, in and beyond the Ingalls' cabin. Most of all, you can join in the warmth and wonderful family life that is tenderly talked about in Laura's book and in this book.

Reading along with Laura Ingalls at her Kansas Prairie Home

Little House on the Prairie is the most famous of all the great books by Laura Ingalls Wilder. There she tells how her family traveled to Kansas and built a log house, how Pa almost died digging a well, how they were almost burned out by a prairie wildfire, and how they faced possible attack from wolves and Indians.

Reading Along with Laura Ingalls at her Kansas Prairie Home goes along with that book, chapter by chapter, event by event –

and tells more about how it really was –

there in 1870 on that Kansas prairie.

Little House on the Prairie deserves more than just a quick read. Such a beloved book stirs thought, reflection and remembering. *Reading Along with Laura Ingalls at her Kansas Prairie Home* does that. Read along with Laura, laugh along with Laura, live along with Laura as we search out the times and spirit of these hardy pioneers. Join in as we stretch out your enjoyment of Laura's book, deepen your understanding of her character, and increase your affection for her wonderful family.

"Oh Charles!"

Homeschool Happenings, Happenstance and Happiness
A Light Look at Homeschool Life

Homeschool pioneers Margie and Dan White reflect on their homeschool experiences from 1976 until today. With Homeschool Helpers, they have held hundreds of homeschool activities and have put out a quarter million words of encouragement. This book includes the top tenth of those writings, everything from homeschooling in the world today to unforgettable family episodes. Such as –

"Eventually, as it always does, truth had to prevail. I had half a hot pink truck. I'm not an overly proud man, I wear jeans and drive old vehicles, and this is really laid back country, but there was absolutely no way I was driving that half a hot pink truck into Hartville."

"With no institutions supporting it, and all of them opposing it, why in the world did homeschooling grow by perhaps 20% a year?"

"We taught all our five kids to read, starting at about age two. We had no idea that they were not 'ready to learn.'"

This book is about family, faith and fun.

Homeschool happenings, happenstance, and happiness!

Tebows' Homeschooled! Should You?
How homeschooling put God back in education!

Tim Tebow is the world's most famous modern day homeschooler. His parents, Pam and Bob Tebow, homeschooled all five of their children. The intense attention on Tim has also put a spotlight on homeschooling. Although practically everyone in the country now knows about homeschooling, the movement still educates only a few percent of the overall student population. Most people are far more familiar with the factory approach to education than this method of individual tutoring.

Tim Tebow's homeschool education was typical of homeschooling in a number of ways. In some ways, of course, his experience was unique. Yet even in that uniqueness he typifies homeschooling, because homeschooling excels with uniqueness. Therefore, there is much to learn about homeschooling in general by looking at Tim Tebow's homeschooling. In this book, we try to draw out those lessons.

School Baals
How an Old Idol with a New Name Sneaked into Your School

If you believe in the God of the Bible, that is religion and can't be taught in the government schools.

If you don't believe in the God of the Bible, that is not religion and can be taught in the government schools.

That is also one of the biggest deceptions ever foisted on any people in all of human history.

Idolatry is not just the worship of an idol, but the exalting of the human spirit against its creator. The same human nature that built Baal and made Molech created the anti-God deception that is taught to nine out of ten young people in America.

School Baals reveals this idolatry in all its duplicity and destruction, and tells you what you can do about it.

Wifely Wisdom for Sometimes Foolish Husbands
From Laura Ingalls to Almanzo and Abigail to Nabal

A Christian wife may be caught between a rock and a hard place. The rock is Christ, the spiritual rock who commands wives to be submissive to their husbands; and the hard place is the husband, who sometimes has less than perfect wisdom. *Wifely Wisdom for Sometimes Foolish Husbands* discusses the pickle of a wife being submissive but still sharing her wisdom with a husband during his few and far-between foolish moments. Such examples include Laura Ingalls sharing her insights with her husband Almanzo Wilder; Ma and Pa Ingalls; and Abigail and Nabal, whose very name meant fool.

This is a sprightly look at a serious subject, when marriage is under attack from all sides as never before. If a wife can share basic wisdom with her husband when he acts like Nabal, then they may save their marriage and rescue their family from destruction. Laura and Almanzo shared good times and bad times, through chucked churns and hot lid lifters, times when she spoke and times when she didn't, times when he listened and times when he didn't, and through all that their marriage lasted for sixty-three years. *Wifely Wisdom for Sometimes Foolish Husbands* may add a few years, or decades, or a lifetime, to your marriage.

Life Lessons from Jane Austen's Pride and Prejudice: *From her book, her characters and her Bible*

Seven characters in *Pride and Prejudice* –

> Mr. George Wickham, with a most pleasing appearance;
> Miss Jane Bennet, who thought ill of no one and who spoke against no ills;
> Miss Charlotte Lucas, who married for position and got only what she sought;
> Mr. William Collins, whose humble abode was so very close to Rosings Park;
> Miss Elizabeth Bennet, with her consuming search for a man of character;
> and Mr. Fitzwilliam Darcy, who helped her find him –

These seven characters in *Pride and Prejudice* present seven aspects of human nature and the consequent complications of obtaining character, in portrayals that were carefully planned and scripted by Miss Austen. *Life Lessons from Jane Austen's Pride and Prejudice* examines Jane's purposeful plan, searching out the depths of her memorable personalities, and seeking the profundity of her meaningful lessons in life, in morality, and in young love.

Fans of both the *Pride and Prejudice* novel and the movies who appreciated Miss Austen's strong moral values will appreciate this easy flowing study of her comedic characters and her Christian character, making a great love story even better.

Daring to Love like God
Marriage as a Spiritual Union

The Love Dare© program, made famous in the movie Fireproof©, was for people whose marriages had problems, to dare them to take steps to better those marriages. Daring to Love like God is the next step, for people with good marriages, who are not about to split, who love God and each other, and who want to grow to become a true spiritual union.

This is one of the great miracles in creation: two people, with different abilities, personalities and wants, who become one, with each other and with God. If you want to be challenged to the very best marriage, Daring to Love like God leads you up that path.

Printed in Great Britain
by Amazon